ASSER OF SHERBORNE

By the Same Author

Georges Vandine: a novel, revised edition 2011

Your Skyward Eyes: a poetry collection, 33 bird poems and others 2011

Openings and Endgame: a collection of 14 short stories 2013

My name is Max: a novel with photographs by Chris Redgrave 2014

Four exits to Smolensk: a novel in four parallel worlds, revised edition 2015

Bernard Parkes: a novel, revised edition 2016

Lavretsky: a novel, revised edition 2016

The Finder of Faces: a collection of 24 short stories 2017

A number of poems have been set for piano and voice and performed in concerts

Several stories from *Openings and Endgame* have been broadcast by the BBC

Letters to my Niece: a play in nine letters, performed in Holywood, Belfast, N. Ireland October 1995 by The Holywood Players

Asser of Sherborne

AN INVENTION

by

Richard Cutler

2009 – 2015

2017 Edition

Proofing and editing by Ann Cutler
Photographs by the author
Illustration by Chris Channing
Revised Version 2018

Copyright © Richard Cutler

First published in 2018 on behalf of the author by
Scotforth Books (www.scotforthbooks.com)

ISBN 978-1-909817-38-8

Typesetting and design by Carnegie Book Production, Lancaster
Printed in the UK by Jellyfish Solutions Ltd.

Whilst this is a work of imagination the shadows,
thin and light, fading and darkening, come from a light source –
the biography of Alfred by Bishop Asser, his spiritual guide
and tutor to his children.

The setting has been in the author's head since he was detached from Somerset at the age of seventeen. The severing as a result of deaths was like a splinter lodged in a finger too deep to be removed. It has caused an unhealed fracture, a narrow door that time has not fully closed.

Contents

AD 892	1
Emma	3
Ring of Rome	9
Emma of Egypt	13
John Saxon	18
An unholy place	23
Punishment	27
Towards a trial	35
Aller	41
Abbess	47
Trial	56
Mons acutus ... Montacute	69
Second medical miracle	77
The afflictions of Alfred	83
Emma's confession	92
No story	96
Author's notes and thoughts	99

ONE

AD 892

My visitors are expected. I have a few moments. I am writing this journal as a man who has reached a great age, but not yet as old as the Master of memory, learning and literature, St Bede of Jarrow. The great saint died near the time of my birth and stands forever as a shining light and example to us all, especially to those of us who have written books and try to continue. I am a man blessed many times over – I am well even at my age, I can walk briskly and good distances and for these gifts I thank God in His enduring mercy and indulgence of an uncertain servant. Also I am well thought of in my house of fellow brothers, and my king is kind to me beyond imagination. I serve God first and then a king so exceptional it is God's hand and miracle that he was born. A gift from heaven.

These pages written in a bleak, bitter winter are not exclusively about Alfred but exist as an exercise for my mind and memory, and to enjoy once more the feel of the quill in my hand. It is a staff to lead me out of this endless cold and half-darkness. Yet for all that, despite the wet, the ice, the risk of falling and the cutting winds from the north and east, I have already begun again my daily walks. There is no town, village, monastery or church that I have not visited during my tenure here – seven years abbot and bishop.

I am the first to admit, to concede that I came here reluctantly. I was on trial, plucked from my lovely Welsh home by the sea to answer a summons, to be judged, to see if I was man fit enough, scholar and teacher, to be tutor to a king's children. One of these pupils, Alfred's daughter Aethelgifu, is to come here this morning. I am Welsh. I am from St David's – it was hard, a bitter departure, to leave behind friends, family, my uncle who has been a father, everything I had come to love, my world. Yet now I have embraced Wessex. I love this land and its rolling downs, the wide skies and the calls of the plover, the over-hovering of kites as large as our Welsh eagles, I love being so close to the memory and afterlife of our Roman educators; I have never judged them like some men of Wales as invaders and occupiers. Four hundred years is not an occupation but an integration. They remain everywhere, in our laws, our roads, our remaining villas and farms, in the very names we see and do not translate – Marston Magna, Marston Parva ... and has not Alfred himself been twice to Rome?

TWO

Emma

This is the second ember day of Lent, a Wednesday and we are fasting, as we shall be also on Friday and Saturday. Today we are much occupied in prayer and quietness. For my visitors it is a bad day for a journey, the lanes are deep and treacherous, the wind and ice cut into the face. Spring is late. It does not seem to want to come and lift us out of this endless cold, the depressing greyness and melt the snow-banks. Two women; one on a white horse covered with a royal blue sash. The other is intriguing – she is coming to me on an older animal, drawn forward by a halter from the leading one. I am watching them through my window. Aethelgifu is a tall, handsome woman, an abbess, so changed from when she was a girl and a good pupil, but the other … what can I say about her as I look down? I have never seen her before, a woman neat and boy-like with cropped hair and no head-covering despite the harshness of the weather. Sebastian has come and has helped down Alfred's daughter. The other sprang from her pack-horse and bows to him. He's looking up at me now, knowing I am here. Yes … I nod. Bring them up.

I threw a log onto the fire. The women will be chilled. It is a long way, a slow way, and they will have left as soon as light broke into the night sky.

They mustn't stay here long if they want to make the return before dark. Better they should stay the night at our sisters' sanctuary at Bradford Abbas.

I am fortunate to have a friend in Sebastian.

My assistant has been with me for three years, a young man with grace and a presence. I am his bishop, guide and instructor, and he is an attentive student but a slow learner. There have been many scholars who need time to think about all new things that reach them, and for some, memory is a small gift to be enlarged by practice. So it is with him. He never treats me as a bishop and that is why I like him so much. In his slowness there is humour, and in his head and heart there is both sharpness and sincerity. He has come to me from the Irish house at Malmesbury, but of his deeper origins I know nothing. His recommendation – 'a genuine, willing and sincere young man' was enough.

Now he is carefully pushing wide my doors to allow the visiting women entry. His voice pleases me.

"My Lady, the Abbess of Shaftesbury and her maid, Brother Asser." His manner to me is almost like an Essene in its levelling. Our Lord Jesus would smile at that. I stand up and go to them, thank him for his welcome to our guests and for guiding them up.

"Thank you, Sebastian. You may wait outside. I may need you." I greet my two ladies with both hands and pass benediction and a blessing over them. This small woman intrigues me. She is thin and lithe like a tumbler, grave-faced and solemn. Her movements as quick as a goat.

"Well, what a pleasure this is, Aethelgifu, and your young sister in Christ, for both of you to come all this way to see me – in the depths of winter, on such a horrible day." I took them over to the window seats, the window I had been watching from – "But, alas, we are fasting until tomorrow. I'm afraid I can only offer you water." I gave a sigh – some welcome that.

I hurried on "But I do hope you will stay in our daughters' cloister. You won't find them so austere, and they'll give you a proper meal after that bitter journey. You mustn't try to get back to Shaftesbury tonight. It's not safe, and you need some good food inside you, and some hot broth."

I was aware how cold my room must seem to them. A few flickers of flame are creeping round from the base of the pine log I had thrown on. A wiser man would have placed it there much earlier. But the chill will soon be gone and we shall have the sweet-sharp smell of pine oils. My much-loved pupil sat first, spreading her gown. The other one stands beside her. My eyes are drawn to her – a complexion not often seen in Wessex, sallow and curious, as if from Chartres or Rome. I have seen before many such people when I was in Aquitaine. Her thinness is remarkable, like a boy as I said, her shawl across the shoulders is in the manner of gypsies, or a milkmaid. Her eyes are elsewhere – they do not meet mine. She has a presence, distant but assured – not servile, but troubled? She has not the attentive gestures of a lady's maid. A strange companion for a king's daughter – she did not sit but stood quietly beside her mother superior.

I noticed from the first her pendant, a Christian amulet with a scarab, the outline in gold thread of a fish, Chi-Ro. Very rare and unusual and never to be seen around the neck of an English maid-servant. To my eyes it was Coptic; its mystery and misplacement here in Wessex will be revealed this morning. Is that why they have come? Am I to resolve a problem with its origins in Alexandria?

"Will you keep your cloaks on … until the fire burns up?"

Alfred's daughter answered. "For the moment, Asser, I shall. But I cannot ask my friend – she has taken the vow of silence … that is why we are here."

I found my writing slate and chalk. I passed it to the Coptic woman.

"Would you write your name on here please, sister, so that I can address you as I'd like to." She wrote three Greek letters, one of them doubled. I think I can work it out. My Greek is only that taught to me as a child by my uncle in Wales. "Emma? Do they call you that?"

She nodded and looked away. It is hard for her to receive the gaze of a man. This is no ordinary woman – she has a force I am aware of.

"Welcome, Emma, to Sherborne … and you, of course, Aethelgifu – both of you are always welcome, my doors always open. But please, don't try and return today, you're both chilled through. Go tomorrow after a night's rest and some hot food." I looked from one to the other, raised my palms in an encouraging gesture. "Yes? Agreed?" I can see now that I was quite wrong about their ages. The open-faced abbess is half the age of the standing boy-woman who has no breasts or hips. "Let me arrange for you to stay in the convent overnight. Sebastian is waiting outside. Allow me to send him over to tell them. He will run all the way, like Pheidippides at Marathon. But it isn't far. Not the best of comparisons." I smiled at them. Have I not taught this young princess Greek and Roman history? But I'm sure she'd much rather have missed it and run out to play with her brother. I am trying to make them feel more at ease, to relax the tension I can feel. Aethelgifu decided.

"Perhaps that is best, Asser. It was very cold coming here. Emma can come to you herself in the morning." She looked up at the companion she had brought to see me, burdened with a vow of silence. "My friend is the greatest of travellers and used to men of your scholarship and holiness, my Lord Bishop. And other men ... not so holy."

My eyes reverted to the Greek letters on the order-board. This woman is a scholar. She understands Greek. So well educated? I crossed the room to the door and called Sebastian in.

"Run to the convent please, Sebastian and ask Sister Erica to prepare for the arrival of King Alfred's daughter and a woman from a distant land." When I returned to my guests, I saw more words on the tablet, written this time in English.

'Are you troubled by my pendant, Holy Father?'

Now I am receiving the full force of her dark eyes. I shook my head and extended my hand. "No. I, too, wear a strange jewel. This ring of mine. It was made in Rome."

Lady Aethelgifu leaned forwards, nearer to me. "Asser, Emma wishes you to lift the vow of silence from her so that she may better live with us, and speak of all the many things she knows."

I sighed, and did not answer. I knew it would not be simple. How can I lift a vow? Shall I have to take her to my archbishop, Plegmund, in Canterbury, for her confession and absolution? Or must I go to Rome to seek a dispensation from Pope Formosus himself? Yet ... am I not God's vicar in Wessex, his servant for this vast diocese? I am glad I have all night to think about it, a night to pray for My Lord's guidance and His wisdom. A sleep to freshen my mind, a breakfast to give nourishment to my body, a morning's sun to shed some light into my heart. Fasting may sharpen the perceptions, warn the spirit, but it does nothing for my brain. I addressed the maid – companion.

"Where are you from, Sister Emma?"

She took back the tablet and wrote the names of three remote places – Alexandria, Antioch, Padova. Was that the way she came? I, too, have been to Padua and listened to the lectures from their learned doctors. What can have led her to come from the remains of the Roman Empire to a small convent in Shaftesbury? Perhaps that is the least of my questions. A thought struck me. She has passed herself off as a man – for safety and the ease of travel ... it would not have been difficult. But why is it now so important for her to reveal herself and speak out? Has she come here to teach or to confess and travel on? I poured out the chilled drinking water from my glass jug into two goblets and passed them to my visitors.

"I shall give you my answer tomorrow morning, Sister Emma. I need to pray, think and ask for guidance. A vow is not easily cast aside – those for chastity, for taking the veil, for marriage, for faithfulness, for silence, for not tainting the air with reckless words. They are commitments to our Lord."

The flames had burst up from the base of the pine log. The fire flared and spluttered, cracked with a spark cascade. The room was filled with the incense from its oils. Perhaps tomorrow, when I have prayed, I shall be listening to a strange confession. We sat for some time in silence. Our thoughts were broken into by a light tapping on my door. I went. Sebastian. He was flushed and breathless.

"They will be welcomed by Sister Erica. The rooms are being warmed and prepared."

"Then you may lead them over. Slowly and gently – they are ladies. Make sure you look after their horses ... find blankets for them, they must be kept warm and stabled. They will need fodder – hay and oats, and water, Sebastian."

He gave me a reproving look from the top of his eyes. "Our Saviour was born in a stable, Brother Asser. I may not know Him as well as you do, but animals – leave them to me. I have lived with horses!"

I dismissed him. I don't mind his cheek, but not in front of guests, and one is a king's daughter. "Just you go and make sure you look after them all properly. You'd better sleep with the horses. And you may bring

Sister Emma to see me in the morning, at ten. I may even let you sit with us – you may learn something!"

He escorted them back to the old cloisters. I was left disturbed and unsettled. I have been brought a very different kind of penitent.

Three

Ring of Rome

hursday; this is not an Ember Day – we are permitted to break the fast. My mind and thoughts were far away when a tap on my door startled me.

"Ah … please come in Sebastian." My friend and pupil enters carrying my breakfast tray. No smile for me. "Good morning … how did you sleep?"

"Sleep? In a stable, Brother Asser?"

He has a fine sense of irony. I like that. "I'm sorry, but we do have a duty to our guests." I am at my window table, he sets down the tray. "Thank you."

This is a meal I have tried to put out of my mind. It is not in the spirit of fasting to be thinking all the time of the next morning's breakfast. Yet there is no denying it is a real pleasure. My bowl is sending up plumes of steam – porridge, honey and goat's milk. Our bees, our goats – only the oats come to us from the miller on the Yeo near Ivel. Sebastian moves it in front of me with a basket of warm bread and salt butter. There is also a beaker of cold spring water. It is a blessing from God that our spring neither dries up in high summer, nor freezes in this unremitting cold. Sebastian is in a silent enigmatic mood. Perhaps his blood was chilled in the Bradford stables. I shall have to try and cheer him up – but I am aware it wasn't I who had to spend a freezing night alongside horses. His turn for better things will come – I shall not survive many more winters and I'm preparing him to be our next abbot. Whether he will be chosen as a bishop only God knows.

He will decide and call him to it if it is his destiny.

"So, Sebastian … what news do you have for me? What have the brothers been saying this morning in the dining room?" He purses his lips as if my questions are too banal and obvious to require an answer. Have I been too indulgent with this young man? He has moods and mannerisms.

"Everyone is talking about only one thing – Lady Aethelgifu and the Frankish woman with her."

"Oh? So they are saying they know where Sister Emma comes from?"

"It's obvious. Anyone can tell from her skin she's from the south of France."

"Really? Men of quick judgment, it seems. I hope your canvas is wider than theirs, Sebastian. How can they know she is not from the countries of Africa? Or from Syracuse ... or the islands of Homer? Whatever, I hope you looked after them properly last night."

My apprentice is surveying me with scorn. What can I have done to earn this man's irony?

"I spent all night with snorting horses. What more do you expect me to do from there?"

"Good. That is why I trust you." I crossed to the water-bowl on my window ledge and rinsed my hands before eating. "I want you to bring the Frankish woman to see me this morning – in about an hour – after my breakfast and prayers. Show her in here ... and you may sit with us. A bishop cannot see a young woman alone in his rooms. And tell me, as you seem to know a lot ..."

He interrupted me. "I know about horses, not women. Or any of the book facts you know."

I let it pass. It was harsh of me to punish him with a bitter night beside snorting horses. "She has asked me to lift from her a vow of silence. I am telling you this in the utmost confidence. None of this must pass your lips in the dining-room. I want to know what you think." He flushes, pleased that I had spoken of such a delicate thing to him, offended by the way I framed it. At first he said nothing – perhaps I had upset him. Perhaps he will not disclose his thoughts to me. Yet he does have a wisdom – a simple and straight-forward kind of common sense I value and have need of.

"You're a bishop. I am only a man who sleeps with horses and brings you breakfast – and empties your bucket."

"Enough of all that. Answer me, I have need of your opinion of what you would do. A vow is a serious matter, taken before God. It is not lightly lifted."

"You're asking me, what I would do?"

"Yes."

He is hesitating and walks to the end of my table to look out into the hills beyond. His gaze is clear, free from the morning's grumbling and hard-done-by complaining.

"Brother Asser ... I would do this. Lift her vow to you only. Then you can find out why she set it."

"Thank you. Sometimes, you see, you are wiser than a man three times your age. What jam are you going to bring up, Sebastian? I think I would like some this morning. I'm in the mood for jam."

He smiled for the first time. "It's not only the Frankish woman the brothers are talking about this morning. They're delighted with the new gooseberry jam."

"There you are, then."

He leaves me with a lighter step than when he arrived. I have hopes for him – he carries a natural authority which the church in England has great need of. Only ... he is still rough at the edges.

While I wait for the so-called Frankish Emma, I feel the need to introduce myself to you better. I would like to say something about the history of this ring on my finger while the first log of the morning catches. I don't want my guest to be cold – she'll be used to much warmer lands than our ice-bound Wessex.

This ring – as I turn it towards the rising flame it flickers as if it were alive. It was made in Rome and came to England on the hand of another bishop. St Germanus. He was, like our own Alfred, a gifted and exceptional man, trained as an army commander before being baptised into the faith of Christ, and then took holy orders. When he arrived from Rome on his mission to the English, he found himself in the middle of a war. An invading army of wild men, the Picts from the far north, had swept down spreading death and mayhem with every march they made, until the great battle of 429, the 'Hallelujah Victory'. There the English warband under the leadership of Germanus put them to flight. He outwitted these ferocious marauders trapping them into an ambush. They never returned. As a mark of gratitude to one of our leaders on that terrible battlefield, a Roman veteran by the name of Sextus Quinctillius Flavus, he presented him with the very ring from his own finger, to mark and give thanks for the man's outstanding courage and leadership. Then a mystery – what happened to my ring afterwards? Who wore it during those decades before the arrival of Augustine?

Finally the ring was brought out of Wessex to Wales, to the beautiful cathedral at St David's where I was born. It was given to me by my uncle when I left my family to serve the king of Wessex, a king already revered and known as a great and learned man. A ring that had continued its life in these fair islands was returned to Wessex. The completion of a strange circle. The passing down of this jewel to me lays upon me a wish, a desire, that one day I also will hand it on to Sebastian, and perhaps then in the second millennium it will carry its great history and provenance into a wiser age. The ring and the faith it represents is indestructible. The ruby set in the central mounting astonished even the Pope himself when I was anointed and appointed to serve as his vicar here in Christ. I shall return to my story, but not now – Sebastian is knocking on my door with a new-found firmness. He feels the day has laid upon his shoulders a greater significance than has yet entered his short life.

I go, open the door and admit him with his charge, the Egyptian novice.

FOUR

Emma of Egypt

I have my chair near the fire though the room is less cold now and the log is burning brightly, hissing and spitting, giving out an aroma that clears the breath and head, that of pine woods. The sun is up – a light and warmth penetrates my windows, filling our little world with hope and promise of spring. Sebastian stands near the door: he is sensitive except when protesting, tactful with everyone except me, and knows he had been brought into our presence as a privilege and learning moment, that he must shrink into the shadows, a man of silence and respect.

The Frankish sister sits on my window chair. Half her face is touched by the dusted sunbeams; she does not look at me directly. There is a depth and enigma to this self-possessed woman that intrigues me and draws me in. Her age is hard to make out – older in the darkness around her eyes, younger in the thinness of her body, boyish in her cropped hair and movements. Her movements are quick, like those of a mountain goat – neat, supple and sure-footed. She looks out of my window as if reluctant to be sharing a room with two men, yet I know she has come to me for something that troubles her deeply. I am impressed – she has the colouring of a woman burned by a desert sun, who may have walked behind trading caravans – a lightness of step but not, I suspect, of spirit. I have seldom seen such woman before, never in Wales, never in Wessex.

It may seem strange and lacking in manners that we remain in silence for many minutes. Nor was there any movement. I sit still in my chair, an ageing bishop, Sebastian is motionless at the door, waiting for a sign from me. Yet for all that, he has a life of his own that does not embrace waiting and has a stillness that comes to him naturally, a gift from God and his mother.

I know the woman in my presence cannot speak and is alert, waiting for me to make an opening, yet I feel this delay is needful. The question is not yet fully stated and we need time for it to pass between us, unspoken, that it may find its own form before being expressed as words and counter-words.

Many questions are damaged and diminished by urgency. The request she has carried with her for so long and so far cannot be resolved and unravelled in any instant judgment. We require the soul of the past, the spirit and ambience in this old monastery of Aldhelm and a silent prayer for wisdom. I believe already that this woman is familiar with loneliness, the separations which divide us – and understands why most of us need to be in a supporting and loving community like the one we have here. Closeness, love and privacy are fruits of the same branch.

Of course there are shepherds, the manuscript copyists, poets and the like who spend most of their lives alone, who choose the other way because it draws them nearer to God, to hear His voice in the decoration of a text, to feel His presence among the sheep, His song in a phrase which flows from the sharpened quill onto the vellum. For the rest of us with duller ears and nearer sight, we need the presence of others close by, so that we are not alone. I shall not hold this silence any longer.

"Sister Emma, to give up a vow is not an act you can do lightly, and I understand that. I am glad you have come to me, but I cannot lift it easily, not a vow of any kind – and the one of silence is a profound one. I shall need to know why you embraced it in the first place. There are some bindings which last forever ... a swan will not change her mate and may die upon his death. A married woman may not change her husband – yet we do permit it ... but not before much careful thought in allowing an overwhelming reason."

She is now looking at me; I have her full attention. What mystery and history lie behind those dark questioning eyes? I continue.

"Under the laws of my king, King Alfred, a man may set aside his wife if she has abandoned him for five years, and he may then take another woman." I paused for she has looked away. Her gaze gave me permission to hear her request, but that moment has passed.

"Men and women are too frail to have any vow laid on them forever. Five years is a long time, yet we all know when even that was not enough ... when Odysseus returned from Troy. But now we live in less revengeful times. Thanks be to God and our Saviour Jesus Christ."

She wears a cross – and understands. I spread my hands in grace. "You have come to me and have found a welcome in your Abbess's house ... I have prayed all night for the Lord's guidance. I believe He has brought you to me for a purpose – and I shall give you an answer."

Once more I have her steady gaze, yet her mind, her eyes and her face are unreadable. She listens closely, intently, but is unable to speak through her vow. I look to Sebastian ... do I see a nod? Does my pupil approve and agree? Surely I must smile at that. I turn back to my Frankish suppliant.

"Emma, there is so much I do not know about you. I am like a court reeve who has to decide a case without any evidence being offered by either side." I know she understands my words. This is a highly intelligent woman who speaks many languages – yet I would not address her in Latin. "I cannot lift your vow of silence until I know much more."

Now I feel she is detaching herself, looking out of my window and upwards into sky which is losing the sun behind grey cloud. Both she and the day are becoming sadder. Her attention has left me. Her shoulders are lower, her head not so assured, so alert. Her presence is blunted. This woman is taking herself to some other place, another time, when whatever happened to her was bad, and silencing. I am aware of her pain and silent language.

"Therefore, Emma, I say this to you. My decision before my pupil Sebastian who is discreet and our witness is as follows: I lift your vow in these three ways ...

Firstly, the release from your vow is temporary; I shall decide finally later.

Secondly, I allow you to speak, but only to me. Sebastian will be with us but you must address no remarks or comments to him.

Thirdly, I must hear – like my king, Alfred, when he decides appeals sent up to him from the plebian courts – your story, your reasons for taking the vow of silence and why you now wish to renounce it. If I see it is the path of your destiny, that it is God's hand behind you moving you in that way, and if I am convinced it is right, then I shall release you from your vow entirely."

Now she is looking at me with eyes full of tears. Have I been too harsh, too pompous, too like a bishop? The woman before me is a person racked by strong emotions and has much sensitivity. What lies behind her vow, what cruelties or shocks made her choose to withdraw from the world, from speech with her fellow beings – other women, children ... and men, I have yet to discover – but will it help her to reveal all those things that happened so long ago, to unburden herself of past sorrows and assaults ... to confess? All my life I have been in God's sight – I do not always please with what I do, or say, or think. But am I not also a man of feelings like this silent beseeching woman touching her mysterious Coptic cross. And what lies deep within me, unexpressed and only read by my Creator? What judgment shall I come to? I have no claim to wisdom but have lived long, read and thought much, prayed often. The young are much more certain – like my friend Sebastian who says he knows more about horses and animals than women. Neither of us is wise – I am a bishop with small gifts ... yet I do not believe myself to be wantonly unkind or insensitive.

"Thank you, Bishop Asser."

Are these the first words her tongue has moulded and released from her lips for five years – ten years ... or more? They reach me with an echo of pain. Yes, it is only by speaking she can free herself and cast out her demons, calm her soul.

"I want you to come to me once a week at this time. I shall listen. We shall move on slowly, not too much at a time. It is not good to hurry, to rush into the past. Think how long a day is ... the past is a distillation of hundreds of days. It needs to be poured out with care, for it may burn."

Her eyes are down. I continue. "I want you to stay with my friend the Abbess Erica where you are now. I shall ask Sebastian to escort the Lady Aethelgifu back to her own house in Shaftesbury."

"When do I start my story, Bishop Asser?"

"You may start this morning. From the beginning. That is the only way. I am sure you were not born in a cold country like ours ...?"

She sighed but did not answer, or do as I asked – begin. And who amongst us can ever know where a beginning is or when an end is reached. Then after a silence came these chilling words.

"I was born in Brittany, and sold into slavery."

No more, not then – we were all shaken and alarmed, shocked by a hammering on my door – an invasion as fierce in its crashing blows as the thudding of my heart in my chest.

"Open up ... open up ... murder! An act of murder! Unholy ... unholy!"

FIVE

John Saxon

 horrendous and shocking crime, and in a holy place – desolate in the middle of marshes. I am waiting for my horse to be brought – and Emma's. I am profoundly shocked – a violent crime against a priest, an attack upon their abbot, a scholar and leader of Alfred's religious house at Athelney. By all accounts this was a savage assault upon John Saxon in his own chapel, before God's altar. Such defiling, desecration – so brutal …

I am astonished at what is happening now with my Frankish Emma. She has told me about a box. It seems it travels with her and there are things in it that may help John if he lives that long. She has gone down for her horse and will ride to the convent for this vade-mecum which clearly has medical contents. I can see this woman from the ancient world has much to teach us, and many surprises. Thankfully God sent her to us in this hour of need – with secrets from her Paduan masters? Yet, have I not been there myself and heard some of their lectures? Yet even there not one of them can understand Archimedes – and as for our remote Wessex, barely half a dozen scholars retain the skill to read and understand Latin scripts.

I am thankful that today there are no marsh mists – the way to Athelney is treacherous. Many a good man has vanished forever in the maze of those swamps.

The island of Athelney rises above the endless marsh. The monastery roof and the church tower are landmarks for any unfortunate traveller – but not in a mist, not in a sea-fog, not in the deepening dusk. For us, there is a firm way which will take us as far as Langport. I have sent Sebastian on ahead – he will run the 25 miles in less than three hours … he's a fine athlete. I've loaded him with strips of sun-bleached linen to arrive well before us. I pray we shall get there in time to help my dear friend John. He's a strong man but our messenger says he is bleeding freely and they do not know how to stop it or how to close a gaping, gushing wound. Praise be to God that the thrusts were not into his heart.

We are now assembled. My horse is a large quiet animal, strong and sure-footed; I shall not ask him to gallop along that treacherous way. John Saxon's life is in God's hands, in the wrappings of Sebastian's bands, and he is held in our prayers.

We ride out. I am in front, Emma close behind. This marsh-way is familiar to me – I have walked it many times. We pick up first the old route to Ilchester, cross the Fosse Way, continue along it as far as Langport then join the Pilgrim Path into the swamps. It is a well-known, well-trodden track taken by pilgrims travelling to Muchelney and beyond – the track taken by my king in those bitter days of retreat and hiding, to the shelter of Sedgemoor – a desolate and deceiving land inaccessible to the Danish raiders.

I cannot tell you how much this outrageous and heinous crime has shocked me. It injures me deeply – such a brutal attack upon a holy, defenceless old man. This is an age not without its evils – Alfred's brother taking the marriage bed of his dead father and fornicating with his step-mother Judith. Now we have a rising darkness from men's primitive minds. But this is not evil – there is nothing supernatural about this callous event. It will have the usual explanation – envy, revenge and utter heartlessness. And cruelty – all vices our Lord Jesus warned and preached against in his message of love. Violence ends nothing, begins everything. What are the winds fanning by a fire of this kind? There have been troubles in Athelney since its foundation – monastery, church and fortress. It is a place no one has ever wanted to come to – wet, cold and in summer full of the marsh-fever. Why-ever did Alfred found it there? Was it to praise God for his safe passage to a shelter after defeat in battle … in his hour of need? Did he perhaps intend it for himself – somewhere to come to when exhausted by the kingship that rests heavily on his shoulders? A safe place from Danes, Devils and Despair?

This is a wind that fans embers. Athelney is a community of Franks. No English monks would come here. It is a sad fact that monasticism is no longer the force it was ... modern times, new ways. Only Alfred loves this place we are hurrying towards. Its very loneliness appeals to him – in the heart of the Levels, marsh on every side, some brackish, half salt where the sea was once driven in by fierce storms.

My king had a monastery built and then found he had no monks to people it, to consecrate it and make it holy. His next mistake – and I say this to his face for he is a listening friend – was to send to France for his monks. Had we been approached earlier at St David's, we would have found Britons for him – Celts used to the solitude of mountains and bad weather. In the event, when the request finally did come, we sent down a small group of holy scholars and what did they find – Franks! Arrogant and uncouth – these were men who never washed, spent their time in dispute and arguing, and were tainted with proud disobedience. Moreover they only spoke their own language. What a nest of vipers. And what a place to send John Saxon to – a gentle man of quiet scholarship and devoted to prayer. They resented him from the beginning, not only for being placed over them but for coming from Saxony. Now he has been cut down by swords in front of his own worshipping altar. This is a hideous crime. Blood has been sent flowing across a holy place. Alfred will punish them severely, by death for the murderers.

"Keep close to me, Emma. Now we are beyond the Fosse Way we must be careful – keep a sharp watch for the way. Very soon this will not be a place to become lost in ... miles and miles of marsh with no landmarks." She brings her horse up. We move on more slowly now. Sebastian will be there tending to John and will bind him up firmly where he can. "Unfortunately Emma, this was a crime waiting to happen. I blame myself, their bishop, for not having foreseen it and acted ... an unruly and disobedient monastery, so far from the teachings of Our Lord."

She has fallen behind me now and I can say no more. The death penalty; there are few capital offences remaining now. We settle disputes with Alfred's Laws and blood feuds are a thing of the past. But in this crime I foresee no mitigation. It will be judged with the same outrage and severity as an attack upon the king himself. The only possible clemency will come if we are able to save Old John's life. My mind is overactive and I must concentrate on our way through these unwelcoming, repelling marshlands. Here, where the track widens as we join up with the old Langport Road, the Roman Road, I call Emma up again. We are able to quicken our pace on this half-paved surface and urge the horses forward in a jog-trot. I need to ask her this question which has been buzzing through my head like an unwanted fly.

"Emma, what can you do to help my friend John if he should be – God preserve him – still alive when we get there? You know that by now he should have Sebastian's bonds wound tightly around him."

I am amused at the way she rides astraddle her horse like some latter day Boudicca. It would be unseemly if we were not alone and hurrying forward on a mission of mercy.

"I shall do what I can, Asser." She looks away. A man's gaze, even that of her bishop, companion and confessor, unsettles her still. I suspect that she has suffered at the hands of men – a child sold into slavery. I barely hear her answer above the clip-clop of our horses hooves on the ancient track-way. It throws up an echo, as would have come before from the rhythmic marching of a legion's boots all those years ago. What comes to me is faint, almost as a whisper might.

"I have worked on battlefields before."

"Ah ... how merciful! God has sent you to us for this day."

I am worried and apprehensive – the journey is taking us longer than I thought. In fact, we do not reach Athelney until late afternoon with our horses tiring, the way frozen where the trees have arched themselves over preventing any sun-heat from melting the ice. Our horses have slipped often, but Thanks be to God, have not gone down. The cold of this day has penetrated deep within us and the light is already withdrawing. Such a brevity of daylight at this time of year, and as we enter the wetter parts of the Levels, a thin mist rises from ditches and drains settling a white hoar-frost on our garments.

We give a prayer of thanks for our safe guidance as we see at last the church tower and monastery roof swing into view. And there is

Sebastian, running hard to meet us, a pair of white-throated ghosts on horseback.

"Brother Asser! I was beginning to think you would never get here! A priest lies dying yet you travel so slowly like some called-in cattle, as if nothing mattered!"

He is upset. I let his words pass. "Is he alive?"

SIX

An unholy place

ebastian throws up his head and shakes it – gives a long sigh. "Barely."

"God be praised. He is merciful."

"I have wound him round with the strips you gave me. Blood was everywhere. His wounds, Brother Asser, are mortal. But you are in time, just, to hear the poor man's confession and say over him the last rites."

I am shocked, dismayed, distressed ... but he is alive.

The chapel must have been scrubbed and set straight. John Saxon was lying on a rush mat where he fell, swathed in bandages dark with blood. The old priest's eyes were aflame with anger. My friend and Brother in Christ did not have the look of a man shrouded for burial or burning – yet he wore a deep pallor, as white as the frosted tracks we had come along. This man is now too angry to die, the voice strong, the accent thick.

"This is an obscene thing, and within my own church, Bishop Asser ... I must not be left here, it is not right, a wounded priest in Christ's Presence – but I cannot drag myself outside. My brothers will not move me. Let me die outside if that is God's will. The ice will finish me off better than any Frankish sword!" He looked away. Through his rage and irony I see pain, a final agony, not yet inviting the throes of death... the pain from his wounds, the agony in his mind and heart. I lifted the limp hand and made over him a benediction, blessed him for all the good things he had done – asked Our Lord Jesus to forgive him for his lapses, beseeched The Father to spare his life and for him to be allowed to finish God's work on earth – a good and loyal servant. I pressed his hand firmly.

"John ... I have with me a woman from Padua who has worked with the wounded on battlefields, but she cannot speak with you for she has taken the vow of silence." I set down his hand. "You must stay where you are. Your brothers were right. I authorise it." I brought my companion forward. The sight before her would have blanched the most hardened warrior, not a sight for any woman. She removed her gown. Beneath she wore only a thin tunic into which she tucked her Coptic pendant. Drawing me to the side she whispered.

"Asser ... I shall need buckets of clean water, salt and a charcoal brazier."

I turned to the stupefied monks standing open-mouthed behind us, shaking their heads, wringing their hands, muttering prayers and chants for the passage of their abbot's soul.

"Off you go! We don't want you gawping and moaning – someone bring us clean drinking water and another coals from your kitchen fire, in a brazier. And be quick! And we need a basin of salt ... Go!"

They looked from one to the other in shock and disbelief at being dismissed from the presence of their dying abbot, life struck from him by murder, doomed and bound for the limbo of purgatory and perpetual night. They were as pale and dazed as the victim, shocked by the flow of blood before the altar, the oozing purple strips of windings, shocked at being in the presence of a woman who had ordered fire and water – devilish things. But they obeyed. Before long three of them reappeared bearing pails of clear spring water, the casket of salt and another with glowing embers.

The Egyptian woman unrolled her bag. Such a sight; never before have I witnessed anything remotely like it, not in Auxerre, Milan or even in Padua itself. Her instruments shone as if for torture – prongs and probes, thin ivory needles straight or gold ones curved, silver salvers, packs of cotton squares of all sizes, some as small as a child's nail, others as wide as a ploughman's hand, lanks of twisted horsehair. And the dreaded clamping scissors, for the fearsome stone that blocks the passage of urine. A terrifying, sickening sight.

"Lord protect us. Emma ... wherever did you get these instruments of magic?" I was so taken aback, an educated man who once himself attended Roman lectures in the doctor's art and craft. My voice half-whispered is of wonder. She did not answer. A strange absorption had entered her, as if she were in the presence of some matter rare, as if occupied by the spirit of the great Hippocrates himself. I was in the company of a woman extraordinary.

She poured some water into a silver bowl, rinsed her hands and then undertook the task of unwinding the bandages from the old priest's neck and chest. He submitted to her fingers, and to her touch and care, like a suffering, injured creature – eyes shut. He sucked in his breath and lay there as motionless as a maid in a faint.

I was sickened by the wound she revealed – a long deep gash along the side of the neck oozing dark spent blood. With the left hand she took a small pledget of cotton in one of her probes and with the right hand passed a silvered rod into the blue flames from the coals until it glowed red. She then worked her way down the gash beside the pounding blood tube alongside, dabbing and burning, sealing every weakness that oozed blood, re-heating her rod from time to time and changing her cotton pads as they became soaked. I was no longer the sickened observer but became entranced, as if becoming a student watching the skill of his master. All around us rose up the defiling smell of burning flesh like some ancient temple sacrifice. There was no doubt the chapel was awash in pollution and would have to be purified, rededicated. Yet the work going on before my eyes was no different from that of Christ healing the leper, or the raising up of a Lazarus. The cavity of the gaping neck wound had become dry, the bleeding silenced and contained, an act not of profanity but of mercy and healing. The old man had fainted, was not of our world, yet remained alive. He could feel none of this.

"Abraham!" I called out. "God be praised!"

She began mixing the spring water with salt until it became as water from the sea itself then irrigated the wound until it was as clean as the rose fingers of dawn-rise at Troy. Patroclus would not have died in the armour of Achilles had this astonishing wound-mistress been there to sew up his mortal cuts. For this was what she was preparing to do next, threading her needles and soaking them in her dish of brine – the gold needles shaped like the crescents of the Spanish Moors. She worked fast, taking each threaded needle in her scissors-clamp and thrusting it through the wound-edge, drawing the gaping cavity together like a queen's first seamstress. Each stitch was pulled tight, flicked into a knot and cut with a glass edge. So neat. Old John's neck was sewn up from top to bottom, as tight as a sack of a miller's best grain, the stitching neat as that adorning a pallium from Rome.

The woman battle-surgeon, Emma, worked rapidly and ceaselessly healing the lesser gashes in the same way. I called for rushlights and oil lamps. The day had left us but the night was softened, lit by a full moon. I ordered tallow flares and more lamps. Emma worked on quickly, not pausing except to move the lights closer to the wounds. Her craft is that of a dressmaker, her fingers those of a Welsh harpist – a miracle to behold – her mind is locked into the task with the subtlety of a mathematician, the inwardness of a saint, the sureness of an archer. If I counted a hundred stitches it would not even then have been all. The woman worked without pause or hesitation until the midnight hour was called by the church sacristan. Suddenly it was all done and she was washing her instruments, drying and smoothing them back down into her Hippocratic roll. John Saxon opened his eyes. In all that time he had not uttered a single cry, a single sigh. I laid a blessing and benediction upon his forehead, the sign of the cross. We lifted Old John onto a board and carried him through to the adjoining vestry, covered him in warm sheepskins. I lay down beside him and fell into a deep sleep in which I seemed to see the stars and planets revolving around a single great light.

This was the first healing done by the Egyptian surgeon – and gloriously the patient lived. I surfaced from a profound sleep to find John Saxon's colour had come up – the ice pallor, the final harbinger, had left him. The fingers of death had moved on. Emma was seated on a chair beside him.

"Emma ... how did you learn all this?" I asked the question patrolling and haunting my mind. But a vast blanket of night and nothingness drew me down into the waves of release and forgetting. I was immersed once more before I could hear her answer.

✼

SEVEN

Punishment

This is our last day in Athelney. Then I shall be going back to my rooms at Sherborne and Emma to the convent at Bradford Abbas. We have been out walking while John Saxon sleeps and rests. We are companions. I say little, ask no questions – there will be time enough for that. Yesterday I took her to see the Abbess Hildegarde at Muchelney. There was no conversation, nor could there have been – and as you would expect the abbess was not at ease with a man, her bishop ... or with the wild rumours flying about concerning the miracle which saved the life of her neighbour and holy scholar priest John Saxon. She is in awe and not a little frightened at being face to face with the woman surgeon who had done it. Yet at the same time she is overwhelmed in gratitude for the saving of his life despite her horror and reservations about the Egyptian's magic which brought it about. Hildegarde comes from Frisia, northern Gaul, which is sometimes known as the Netherlands. What do they know there of these arcane matters, or Britain – where everyone hears about and fears the druids. I could see her moving back in her chair and staring at Emma's Coptic cross with deep suspicion. Yet she is a good and kindly woman, severe with her nuns but never unkind. I hope and pray that with the passage of time these women will become friends. They are more similar than widely different.

We stayed on at Muchelney for compline prayers. In my intercession I gave up heartfelt thanks for the restoration by Our Father and His son, through the hand of His servant Emma, of life in Abbot John, for endowing her with these remarkable and unique skills, for the Mercy of Christ in delaying his death, for God's love to each and every one of us, even to those deep in this unholy and callous sin.

It was by then too dark and dangerous to return to Athelney and the moon though full, was fickle and disappeared for long periods behind low cloud and the risen mist. I spent a cold night in the stables with our horses that they might not be stolen, for I had long since sent Sebastian back with the news of the miracle for our brothers in Christ. Was not our Saviour born in a stable? Did not Sebastian himself spend a night twice as cold as this not a week ago in the Bradford stable? I have had the luxury of a warmer wind from the south-west. He will know now that I have done it and have not asked him to undertake something I was never going to do myself. But I shall not shrug, roll my eyes and complain when I tell him.

In the morning I suggested to Emma that we should make the short diversion to Langport on our way home. It is a port formed by the confluence of two rivers, my own river Yeo which rises at Sherborne and the Parrett, a sluggish, flooding waterway. The settlement is on higher ground, up from the old quays – but the importance it had during the centuries of Roman occupation has been lost. Flooding and silting and the neglect of dredging has made the port too shallow – and the sea itself has receded. Yet there remains a community of hard-working folk, free craftsmen, women skilled at basketry and eel-traps, fowlers, fishermen, withymen and small-holders. Here are the best baskets in Wessex, and the boat builders continue with and hand down the ancient design of the flat-bottomed craft for eelers and fowlers, built on these yards since time immemorial. The women also spin a coarse flaxen yarn for sails and floor coverings, and their rushlights are better, longer lasting than in any part of Alfred's kingdom.

Close by is the church at Aller where King Guthrum with thirty of his jarls were welcomed by Alfred in peace-making. The Danish king was baptised and took upon himself a new name, Athelstan. But it was in a poor man's hut, now abandoned and within the marsh, the moor of sedge, that we came across people utterly different. Lepers. I shall return to this – it changed our lives. Only this I shall say here, when I heard the rattles and drumming from beyond the Aller churchyard I was, like the others, overcome with fear. I wanted to hurry away, turn my back – but I couldn't. Emma had grasped my arm and held me back. Surely there is no truer Samaritan in the length and breadth of lands from Wessex to Whitby than the woman whose hand was gripping my arm.

Time to follow events at hand. As I have already said, the events surrounding the lepers are for another day.

For a whole week I have been worried and fearful for my dear friend John. I haven't been sleeping well and have had strange dreams invaded by fevers. I have imagined every disaster visiting my old friend, why I don't know. Is it a premonition? I wake at night picturing him suffering the onset of putrefaction, buboes in the armpit and the thin yellow fluid I have so often seen in the wounded after battle which brings in the rigors and kills the strongest of men. But listen; none of that came to pass. I sent Sebastian over and he came back with this astonishing report that Old John was up and about, scolding his Frankish brothers, shouting and calling them to order. And there have been days of prayer, thanksgiving and revival – the chapel has been scrubbed from top to bottom and re-sanctified with new candles and new linen. Everything else has been burned. Thanks be to God.

My king, Alfred, came to me this morning. He had been to see Abbott John himself and has come back amazed, disbelief at the skill of our Egyptian had he not seen the evidence before his very eyes. Emma is still here, but he couldn't question her because of the vow. He told me he sat for a long time with Old John, demanding to know everything ... but what could he say except that he was alive, his life saved ... the man had been in a faint throughout all of it. I described as best I could to Alfred the events of the entire battle-surgery – it has burned deep into my memory. None of it shall I ever forget. I started with what she'd ordered – the spring water, salt and burning coals, then her instruments ... the sealing probe, the clamps, the ivory needles, the brine, even the hand-washing beforehand. I said how blessed we were to have sent to us at such a moment a woman skilled so highly in the art of battle-healing, physician and lithotomist from ancient Egypt and from the schools of Rome and Padua.

He asked for more – about her life. So many questions. I could say nothing. What will pass between Emma and myself will be for the two of us alone, and God the Father who sent her.

Alfred is sensitive. He understands. We passed on to matters surrounding the evil-doing, the heinous crime, and the utter disgrace that trailed behind it like a stinking corpse left by forest wolves.

"The murderers are in chains, Asser, in the prison cells. What a sorry sight the two of them make, weeping and groaning and shouting out for mercy. They expect me to order their killing at any moment."

"Who are these villains. Two evil and stone-hearted madmen?"

He stood with me at the window looking down onto the forecourt where I had watched his daughter arrive with our Coptic saint.

"One of them, Asser, is young and stupid. He is called Maurice. It seems he was led on and goaded by the older one, Brother Esquith. He was the prime mover. A man embittered and easily roused to anger. They know full well they must be hanged for what they have done – yet, I am loth to do it. You must hear this case yourself, my friend, in a court ecclesiastical – the crime has occurred within a church, our church. Your diocese."

"Me! I should hear this ... and sentence them to death?" The thought shocks and appals me, turns my stomach over. I am not a man of vengeance to order the taking of life. That is not Christ's message. Alfred is smiling kindly. His face seems thinner. Is it in his own sickness that he has no strength or heart to punish these two savages?

"I can think of no better man, Asser. But think of it like this – the young one Maurice is guilty by association. He took little part in the attack. Whatever judgment you impose, you shall have my full support."

"Death?"

"Do you imagine my hands have never killed an innocent man?"

"You are merciful to a fault, Alfred. I shall not hear this alone."

"Nor would I expect you to."

"I shall need two side persons."

"Of course." He came closer to me and laid his hand on my arm. "Let us sit at your table. Enough of this talk of death. I shall tell you what I have done at Athelney."

He nods his head slightly towards me and opens his eyes wider. It is a gesture I have witnessed often – it conveys so many nuances and moods.

"Where's that man of yours, young Sebastian? Bring him to me."

I had placed him at the door; I went over and called him in.

"Sebastian ... your king has need of you."

He came to us, eyes wide but not submissive and made a deep bow with a grace of gesture I did not know he had. Alfred nodded.

"What does your bishop like to drink in the mornings, Sebastian?"

My pupil responded by spreading his hands as if he were already an archbishop, looked at me and pursed his lips thoughtfully. My young friend has missed his vocation – he should have been a wise man, one of the three Magi.

"Warm honey-yogurt with some cream. Sometimes I add some drops of oil of cloves."

"Good. Then bring us a jug of it, please, with two beakers."

When he had left Alfred asked, "How is your young man doing, Asser? Is he a good pupil?"

I had to smile at that. "When he doesn't imagine he already holds high office."

"Ah ... I like that."

I brought a second chair to the table and Alfred explained what actions he had imposed on his ill-placed monastery at Athelney. He sighed.

"Yes... I did make a mistake, my friend – bringing over unwilling and resentful Frankish brothers. Well, I've sent half of them packing – back to Auxerre. They should have never left it in the first place, not to come to some foreign house in so dismal a setting with all that surrounding damp and emptiness. So cut off and cold ... and desolate. Back in their abbey at St Germaine the sun shines every day. It is warm and healthy – there are no mists. There is no marsh fever. I am holding back only ten monks to keep the place alive, and only two of those are Franks who asked me to let them stay on. The others are our people ..." He turned his palms upward and raised his eyebrows, "... from your country, my friend ... Wales. Plus a handful of brothers from Northumbria. The twinned outlying house at Midelney is to be shut. It is a grim and solitary spot – a bleak and unloved place. I shall decide later what use, if any, it shall be put to."

I have walked there from Athelney. Five miles along marshmen's tracks. Just about habitable in mid-summer. "Yes, it is a lonely house, Alfred. Even the Black Friars didn't want it ..."

Just then a tap at the door.

"Come in."

Sebastian with a tray. My Cornish china jug and two engraved glasses. I am not pleased, "Glasses, Sebastian ... with hot milk?"

"I have warmed them, Brother Asser." He turned to Alfred. "Our beakers, My Lord, do not look so well. These have belonged to our founding father Aldhelm."

Alfred looked at him closely. "I see you are a man who thinks for himself, Sebastian. Good, you may pour out your sweet offering. We are more than ready for it."

My pupil is getting himself noticed. He poured the honey-milk from the jug with great care, half-filling only the precious glasses.

"Thank you. Tell me, Sebastian, what do you think of the Midelney House where this great crime had its origins?"

"It is a refuge, My Lord, but not for foolish Franks."

The king gave a faint laugh, so rare for him. "You have a plain-speaking young novice, Asser ... I think we should encourage him." From a waist-purse Alfred drew out a thin, decorated bookmark. "Here, Sebastian, read and mark well. Perhaps one day we may need you to instruct these foolish Franks."

Sebastian was overwhelmed. He looked at me, a deep flush rising into his cheeks, and in his confusion forgot to thank his king. He hurried out.

The sweet beverage was good and flavoured well. We returned to the closure of Midelney Priory.

"Sebastian is right. It is a refuge ... but for whom? The building is firm and dry. Did you know, Asser, it was once a Roman farmhouse. They built to last – thick stone walls, a well ... and once there was a proper fishery. After they left us it gradually fell into disuse – even the hives and the good honey." He sighed. "Don't you think they were wiser men than us? Ten times more literate. I am trying to bring some of that back – my schools, our English language for all ... not Latin for the few ... words that everyone can more easily understand ... because it is spoken. Everywhere. That is my aim, my friend. We need to catch up with our past and honour it."

I escorted him to the gates and watched him ride away alone. He is a great king with an exceptional mind. Alfred has brought us peace for fourteen years, the Danes defeated and pushed back east, Guthrum now a Christian. We are blessed by Alfred's writings, his books and translations, the schools, Winchester cathedral … yet no one can help him with his own afflictions. Pain and darkness descend and ravage him. He shuts himself away until the impenetrable gloom lifts. How can such a good and gifted man be so tormented?

I returned to my rooms and drew the chair back from the table into the window alcove. There the sun shall warm me with its new heat – a rebirth that will draw up the winter-sown wheat and set yellow catkins on the hazels, thrust into longer days the green spears of daffodils. But strange, other thoughts are passing through my head. I am not the same man since meeting the Aller lepers. Our religious daughter-house at Midelney, so despised by the Franks forced to live and work in … might it now be put into some kind of healing use? I have the glimmer of a project; it is as yet unformed and loose. I do not wish to place the souls of two brothers, once monks prayerful and walking the holy life, into Hell. Nor hang them with monastic nooses of their own making.

It is now afternoon. I am walking with Sister Emma. We speak little and see much – a world awakening from the fist of snow and ice and unending winter into hope – hope of a new season and new life. The birds are lively too and calling everywhere to everyone – even the crows have shed their dark threats. For all this, there remains a problem – Erica. The abbess of our sister's house at Bradford is deeply suspicious of our battle-surgeon, of a woman who looks like a boy, rides and strides like a man, who can run like a goat and says nothing. It is small wonder that in that house of women they are wary and unwelcoming. They have placed Emma in a storeroom above the convent scriptorium. She lives, sleeps and sits there in solitude except when she goes out for a walk or comes to me or goes to Athelney to visit her patient. Emma is not admitted into the refectory or allowed into the abbey, or into the chapel for prayers with her fellow sisters. They do not like or understand her Coptic cross – they are unworldly and untravelled women following Christ – and are afraid of it. No words of mine make the slightest difference. Only one thing is in their minds – to be allowed to ask her to leave, but they cannot. She is my guest entrusted to their care and good keeping. They would dearly like her to return to Alfred's daughter's convent at Shaftsbury – her presence among them is unsettling, and unnerving. Moreover they are terrified they have given shelter to a magician and what she did with John Saxon was dark meddling, her surgical instruments the tools of devilishness. They watch all the time for signs and strange symbols. She is forced to take her food with the gardeners, village women and boys who have more common sense and charity. One thing is becoming clear –soon I shall be forced to place her somewhere else. The aggression towards Emma is getting worse – we have had more than enough violence within a religious house. I am acutely aware that I shall have to act so much quicker this time than wait for events to rush forward out of control.

I return alone. The day has left us. My candlelight and oil lamps, the glowing embers of my fire make me even more pensive. Superstition and ignorance abound and are enemies to kindness and progress to better, wiser days.

    I also have upon my shoulders the forthcoming trial of two monks upon whom many shall expect a death sentence to be placed upon them by their bishop. But sleep, in all its mercy is overwhelming me. My Lord and Saviour calms me with His love. May He guide me through these turbulent waters.

✻

EIGHT

Towards a trial

Tomorrow, Friday, is a day of fasting; we are still in Lent. The mornings have become lighter and our afternoons longer. I measure time by the sun, its light and warmth, by the arrival of snowdrops and primroses – and recently with Alfred's invention. He has brought us his measuring device, six water candles which stand in the narthex of our chapel and are lit at sunrise, reset at each equinox. The candle-clock gives us divisions for the day, our prayers and for calling the brothers together for meals. Before this new clock we had no good measure except sundials, hopeless in this sunless winter, and the hourglass turned supposedly by the youngest novice but who never gets to it in time to do the correct inversion. Alfred's mind is never still. His time-measure is a great blessing.

Tomorrow is the day set for the trial of the two Athelney murderers or would-be killers, had not the Almighty Father sent us our blessed and gifted Emma. The two Frankish criminals have been brought here to Sherborne and are in the cellars, in chains, shackled to ring-bolts once used for suspending hams. They are in an abject state, pitiful to hear and behold. Their chains will be removed and tomorrow they will be brought up into the light, into the room we have set aside for the hearing, a court, on a day they will imagine shall be their last. They know full well that their offence carries with it the sentence of death.

I have decided that they shall receive food and water, their chains loosened.

The old man, Brother Esquith, is hard. He can take it all but the boy, Maurice, starves himself in deep penitence, praying and weeping, calling out to God for mercy and forgiveness. But if there is no punishment, laws have no meaning and society is anarchic – and a lawless society is no better than a pack of wolves. Remember that these two men are not from the secular world of craftsmen, freemen, nobles, not even bondsmen or villeins who when they appear on a charge of attempted murder are supported by oath-helpers and a team of kin and sureties. Far from it. These are men in holy orders, committing their savagery in a holy sacred space for which the penalty is death. Yet the king, Alfred, sublime in his mercy, boundless in his understanding, believing himself to be partly to blame, has asked the church to try its own felons. But here's the point – can any bishop acting in the name and spirit of Jesus Christ, Saviour and Light of the World, whose message is love and that a repentant sinner is worth more than the righteous – can His vicar, in Wessex, sign a death warrant? I have need of my level-headed pupil and friend Sebastian. Here is a young man not overburdened by an excess of knowledge and who as yet loses no sleep over decisions, unlike his abbot and certainly unlike his king. Perhaps put it this way – I have heard a small voice of calm. I have been shown a way forward. God be praised, He is merciful. I have been led there not from the home-spun wisdom of Sebastian but by two frail lepers and their grandchild, a thin half-starved girl by the name of Alwyn, who cares for them.

I am waiting for Sister Emma who is to see me today about her wish to have her vow of silence set aside. I must travel through this Minoan Maze with care. If I allow her to speak too freely, it may be her undoing. A shallow drill will bring to the surface a milder tilth for who knows what a deep plough would uncover. I shall need to protect her for the time when she does speak out to an incredulous world – from jealousies, accusations of magic and the taints of wizardry and witchcraft. These bad seeds are already in the air. A wind of wisdom shall be needed to blow them out of reach, over the horizon. Listen, be as shocked as I was ... she has already laid her hand upon a leper. She follows in the footsteps of the Master. Ah ... there are soft footsteps. A tap on my door.

"Come in."

Emma is shown in by Sebastian. He motions her forward and takes up a position just inside the door. I stand to greet her. It is respectful. The abbess Erica and her nuns at Bradford show no respect whatever.

Yesterday they came to me complaining of her remoteness and the way she keeps her distance. They feel they are shunned and rejected. But it is they who do not invite their guest into the chapel and refectory – it is they who have thrown up an atmosphere against her. And it is coming to a head. I cannot ask them to shelter a woman they fear and dislike for much longer. But on the other hand, I am reluctant to allow her to return to Shaftesbury unhelped. And rejected. I have been chosen to hear her out, decide on her plea – I shall pray for a solution. If our Lord and Father and His Son have seen fit that she might now be brought out into a world where so many suffer, then my course is clear. Everything else is secondary.

"Please take that chair in the window, Sister Emma." She does so. In the chair I have placed there for the purpose. Her visit to me is not penitential, though we are still deep within Lent. "It's not your past or your vow I want to speak to you about this morning." She sits quietly and has a remarkable composure, a woman of inner strength. The outwards signs of this we have witnessed already. I was taught a strange and unforgetable lesson. I bring my chair over, one I feel good in – it is made of withies and shaped by the basket craftswomen of Langport. It fits me well. I am alert but at ease. I rest upon its arms and supporting back – except these days my bones are nearer the surface and Sebastian has kindly set in there a cushion. She looks into my eyes then away.

"I am listening, Bishop Asser."

Yes, she would listen at the feet of Socrates himself. We have never before had such a physician in Wessex. A strange thought enters my head. Who has placed it there? Perhaps one day she will direct her gaze and exercise her skills upon my king, upon our troubled Alfred. No doctor has ever been able to diagnose his illness, or lighten his pain – ease his mind that he should sleep like Everyman. This rarest of women has two over-riding gifts; the quickness of a shoemaker in her fingers and a scholar's logic in her mind.

Once again we do not begin for several minutes. I allow my eyes to look over her head and out of the window. Today, mercifully, is less cold and a morning sun shines upon us all a benevolence. I love this season for the sunlight when it comes in and warms even the depths of winter.

Over there, the white-thorn has come out into blossom and behind it a glimpse of yellow – our weeping willow, yellow-green, announcing a new season, a new life upon the iron-iced ground. Its sister almost in touching distance is far more thrusting, a goat-willow already tipped with the yellow and a soft fur of a marmalade cat. A reminder at this moment of that bitter-sweet jar long since gone, made from Spanish oranges and served now in some richer homes as a breakfast jam. Spring is arriving announced by its heralds and harbingers. Our hazel hedges are festooned in catkins and the horse chestnuts have formed their sticky buds. I have in mind for us on such a blessed day a trip back to Aller. I will explain as we go along.

One of the Bradford nuns – before I went out for my walk to be able to breathe sweeter air – came boldly into my rooms in a state of high dudgeon, a carping and protesting woman of little humility. She complained to me bitterly that she had concealed herself and had observed Sister Emma doing magic. It seemed that she had a pan of boiling water and was placing into it her probes and tongs, and the needles she passed through the flames of the fire beneath. The hiding nun, Sister Elizabeth, was outraged at the magical practices, reported it to her abbess and was despatched to me to let me hear this blasphemy first hand. Of course it was nothing of that kind, simply cleaning and caring for her instruments of healing. The woman was in such a state she covered her face with her hands and then pulled down her shawl, fingered her rosary and burst into a torrent of 'Hail Mary'. I spoke severely, ordering her to be silent and to uncover her head. Yet who could blame her – these matters are not only strange for simple uneducated women, but unknown virtually anywhere in England. But – does not the wifely jam-maker first fill her jars with boiling water to disperse the miasma and keep at bay the white and green moulds? At last I drew in my mind; I was on the verge of rudeness in making my disciple of Hippocrates wait so long for me to continue.

"Emma, tomorrow has been set aside for the trial of our two fallen Athelney monks – here, in our refectory ... which we're making ready at this very moment. I would like you to sit beside me at the hearing as the court recorder."

"A woman recorder?"

"Of course, and why not? Nor would you be the first scholar to do so – Alfred has asked his sister, your abbess, to help him before. This is more unusual than his appeals – a crime in a church to be heard and sentenced in a court ecclesiastical. A crime that carries the death penalty. Besides, is not one of the greatest English scholars Abbess Hilda of Whitby?" She is looking searchingly at me. I hurry on. "But today there is something urgent we have to do before the trial. We must go back and meet again your three lepers at Aller. Langport is a longish ride as you know. We must leave soon."

"I do not understand."

"This morning I received an inspiration from Our Saviour and Healer. I feel He has spoken to me. Now go and find Sebastian – ask him to saddle up one of his quickest horses and one for me." I sent her away. Within moments Sebastian was tapping on my door. He could make out nothing from her miming and pointing. I had forgotten about her vow.

"Sebastian, Sister Emma and I are riding this morning to Aller. We need to speak urgently with her lepers. I shall need your horse, it is quicker than mine – and find a similar one for Emma – sure-footed and able to keep up." It is his strength that in times requiring action he does not throw up contradictions or questions. A nod, that is all. "Listen … hurry please – and gather up pots, pans, blankets and clothes for those three unfortunates. I have already opened the alms box," I showed him my purse, the shillings and pence. A fortune for some.

"Make ready two saddlebags – we want to leave quickly – these days are short and we must be back before the light goes. "

I paused, "Something else. While I'm away, I want you to go down to our prisoners, unshackle their chains and give them water to wash in and clean gowns. Have them brought hot soup and yesterday's bread. They will believe this is their last supper, the final meal for their unhappy passage through a life of cruelty and folly. Be that as it may. You shall inform them that their trial begins in the morning. They will appear before a tribunal with their bishop the chairman, the woman surgeon beside me as our recorder, and yourself on my right side – the lay member. We are their judges."

"Thank you, my Lord Bishop. Thank you!" He is affected.

We left quickly – Emma, myself, saddle-packs and two sturdy quick animals.

NINE

Aller

The church at Aller is sturdy. It was well built by our masons and has been a refuge for families and animals in times of storms and floods. It was wisely built on the higher ground out of Langport – but nowhere near as high as at Somerton. It was within the Aller church that the Danish King Guthrum chose the way and teachings of Christ. But this morning we are bound for a more lowly place neither refuge nor holy – a hut. As a dwelling it was abandoned years ago until becoming a shelter for eelers and tenchermen. But after the January floods it was all but swept away – no use for man, beast, fishermen or fowlers. But fit for lepers.

I shall have to take you back to events at the end of last week. We were in the Aller churchyard having walked there from Athelney to preside at a baptism, the first-born child to a family of Langport basket makers. As we arrived with the kin and swaddled baby, we heard in the distance, both before and after the service, the rattles and drummed warnings of the marsh lepers. I had wanted to get away as quickly as possible. I know I'm too old to worry about catching the terrible sickness but the drumming of lepers puts a deep fear into everyone. In the saddest way it placed sorrow and a threat on what should have been a happy event. I turned to leave with the others – we had been invited back by the family for ale and cake – but was restrained by Sister Emma's hand on my arm.

"I need to see those people, Asser."

"Which people?"

"The lepers."

My heart sank. I certainly didn't want to see them. People drifted away from us. In the distance came across the marsh the rattles and tappings which alarm and warn. Leprosy strikes terror into the heart, the disfiguring illness, a sickness where the victim becomes an outcast like a fox with mange or the foaming dog. These are children of Christ bearing and wearing the stains of Cain.

"Nobody sees lepers, Emma. They know that. A touch from them and you are filled with their corruption."

She held my gaze for a long time. "All that, Asser, is ignorance and superstition. I was sent to the lepers in Rosetta. Am I tainted with their corruption?" She shook her head. "No. I have no fear. I am familiar with this illness."

By now we were alone in the churchyard. I looked towards the church where Guthrum had felt and been received by Christ. I also knew that Jesus touched the leper and the man was healed. But here? Our lepers? Warning us to keep away? I took a deep breath. Very well ... we shall walk down and place alms in their begging basket. After that I am in the hands of my Maker. I nodded.

"If that is your wish. Let's walk down to their begging basket, Emma. We shall give alms."

I felt for my purse. I always carry alms with me – I see many sick men, women and children – and babies. Never have I been near a leper.

We go down. I do not lead, she is six paces ahead of me. The baskets are placed on a low wall which marks the edge of the burial grounds and the beginning of spaces outside for those who die by their own hands, for the babies who die before baptism, and those we hang. Standing a stone's throw behind on the far side of this desolate space, drums and rattles silent, watching us with the eyes of a thrashed horse or a whipped dog, are three people. Two are old. Their feet are bandaged, the hands held behind to hide the shame of them. A step ahead of them stands a tall girl, fair-haired and without a blemish. She watches us with a gentle smile, thankful we are bringing alms. I am astonished. Why-ever is she with those two leprous ancients? Is she a vision, a Magdalen who washed the feet of Christ and dried them with her hair? Emma strides past the begging bowls, goes up to the child and takes her in her arms. What am I seeing? Even the Good Samaritan did not embrace lepers. I am deeply shocked. Yet there is the presence of God near us. I place a silver coin into each basket. It must be that the girl looks after the old ones, buys food with the coins thrown. But why? Is she not an Angle, but an angel? Emma brings the girl to me holding her hand.

The old ones stay back ashamed, still concealing their hands. Then they sit together on an old lichened grave-mark.

"Asser, this is the grandchild Alwyn. She is free of the disease. Do not be afraid of her."

I trace a benediction over them both but my heart is racing, with some unevenness. I can clearly see how thin and wasted the girl is, her bones showing. She holds in her face an age far beyond her years. I am shaken and disturbed; if this girl is so unafraid of the disease in her grandparents why am I, at nearly 60 and at the end of my life showing so much cowardice? Am I not praying more for myself than the child. I am speechless – she had a life ahead of her, love, marriage and children, instead she takes up with the most rejected of people, wandering lepers incessantly banging their drums and rattles, to look after them. No greater love can there ever be.

She carries them on her shoulders, in her eyes, across her formless chest, living in huts and hovels and travelling with the stigmata of the worst disease in Christendom. And her own mark of dismissal – the pallor of the bled and fainted, chilled by the bitterness of marsh winds, drenched by winter rains – never dry. An isolation so utterly profound. The warnings they give are mandatory, otherwise they will have village dogs set on them. I am calling upon my soul. Are these three people not also loved by He who made them? Are they not also a part of my flock as God's vicar on earth, in Wessex – my sheep and my brethren? Do I only pray for the souls of the healthy? Her smile is for me, and I am undone by it.

"Is your name Alwyn, my dear? That is a name from my own country. Where are you from?"

"From Caerwent, my Lord Bishop."

"Caerwent ..." I responded with a sigh, a name like her face, so full of the past. I looked to Emma still holding the child's hand. The name of their town moves me almost to tears. What is happening?

"I know Caerwent. I was nursed back to health there many years ago in the monastery."

I hear now my homeland in her voice. "I am a child of the Convent, Lord Bishop. I asked for release to look after my grandparents when they fell ill and were cast out."

"How merciful ... Christ must have called you. I had your nuns come to me when I was ill with their potions and balms. It is a healing order?"

"Yes, my Lord."

"And were you already a Carmelite sister?"

"Only a novice, sir."

"Carmel is the mountain garden of God, Alwyn – oaks, pines, laurels and olives. The monastery on the mountain is called Elias after Elijah. It is sometimes said that Mary herself, the mother of Jesus, was also a Carmelite." I returned her smile. "Bring your grandparents to see me."

"They have the leprosy in their hands and feet, sir, and they speak no English."

I said gently, "But I shall speak to them in Welsh. Would you like to become an abbess, Alwyn?"

She lowered her eyes. "I am too young, my Lord Asser."

"For how many years have you walked about with your kin and kept them alive?"

"Three years, sir."

"For each of your years we may reckon ten of mine. Bring them to me."

Emma and the girl left me. They walked over to the burial stone where the old man and his wife were sitting. I could see at once how reluctant they were to come, terrified of what I might say or have done to them. At last the woman came, each hand held, one by the girl the other by my fearless Egyptian. But she would come no closer than ten paces.

"Welcome. May God's blessing be upon you. I am Bishop Asser, now of Sherborne, once of your country, Wales." The woman looked at me in astonishment, wide-eyed and open-mouthed at being addressed in her own tongue. "What is your name?"

"Ifanwy."

I was moved by the strength of her answer. She was proud of her name – the ring of it, its Welshness. I have that pride too in my own baptismal name Arwel, but it was left behind like a fish stranded after a withdrawing tide. My uncle admitted me into his church, St David's, a child of God he used to say, and I became Asser. "What is your husband's name, Ifanwy?"

"Owen of Caerleon, my Lord Bishop."

I took several steps nearer to her. She was still being held, reassured by the young saintly girl and by Emma. Her head dropped to her chest. Eyes down. I am the worst coward here, afraid to touch her. A force urged me, I reached forward and touched her hair, then traced above her the cross of My Lord and Saviour. *In nomine Patris, Filius et Spiritus sanctus.* God bless you."

I stepped back so as not to frighten her further. "How strange it is that we should meet here. Now. Did you know that St David founded the house in which I was born – that he came up to us from Caerleon?"

"I have heard the story, Lord Bishop."

"And that the nuns who nursed me when I was ill also came from Caerleon, your grand-daughter's house?"

"We all go where we are called, sir."

"Then listen. Go back to your husband and tell him this, that I am founding a new Carmelite monastery with a hospice, not far from here. Tell him that both of you will be placed there to be cared for, that it is my wish. I feel today that the Hand of Christ has been laid upon us all and led us this way. God be praised in all His mercies." I paused and smiled. "Go with my Sister Emma. I have more to say to your grand-daughter."

The old woman fell to her knees, covering her face with her bandaged hands. Emma helped her up and they left slowly. I touched the arm of the thin gaunt child of the marshes.

"Come with me, into the porch of this church."

But she would not walk up at my side, afraid to continue without her drum that she would be set upon and killed. But there was no one.

"Please. I shall protect you. No one will harm you." In the porch I sat on a bench and asked her to sit opposite.

"There, don't be afraid – Christ is with us." I spoke in English as she knew it so well. After a few minutes my composure returned, I took her arm and together we entered the church. It was empty except for the presence of God. Only an hour before it was full of basket weavers, kin and a mother with a new-born baby to be baptised. The candles at the altar were still burning – they threw forward a warmth much stronger than their flames and flickering light.

"Kneel in front of me, Alwyn."

She knelt, head lowered. Her fair hair was gathered tightly into her neck by a scarf and band. I placed my cross around her neck. It hung down in front of her swaying and glinting in the candlelight.

"All Mighty God and your Blessed Son who sees and hears everything and whose compassion has entered Alwyn's heart, who heals and comforts, take this young woman into Your service as Your abbess. She has walked for three years in the wilderness, let her now come out into the light. Nourish her gifts, strengthen her heart and increase her wisdom. Her courage and faith has brought her here before You this day to receive your Son's cross and embrace His healing. Bless her and keep her in Your loving care now, and forever. Amen."

I raised her up and traced a cross upon her forehead. "Sister Alwyn, you shall be the first healing Abbess of Carmel with its hospice for lepers. You are brave, fearless and kind – God has sent you to us in our time of need."

She said nothing but looked away, eyes washed by tears.

TEN

Abbess

ome of you will be wondering when I'm ever going to leave yesterday and get on with today. This is not a story to be rushed. Be patient.

Two horses, a bishop in front and behind him a pack-horse laden and ridden astride by our wonderful disciple of Hippocrates, follower of Aesculapius of Epidaurus, Emma. I am almost into today. Here is a little more ... this is how that day ended.

When I brought Alwyn back after her ordination and consecration to Christ, we found the others just as we had left them, still seated on the ancient burial tumulus on the far side of the outer cemetery. They were bewildered, astonished at the sudden change of events, to see their grand-daughter with Bishop Asser's cross of St Christopher around her neck. I made a blessing over them.

'Marvel at nothing for thou hast borne the whole world on thy shoulders and its sins likewise. Blessed are they who believe in Me.'

The girl held her head proudly and allowed her fingers to touch the cross. What reverence and belief is there within her. The two ancient kin moved back, away from us but I held up my hand to stop them, that they should remain close to Sister Emma. A special moment, for I wished to present my new abbess. I touched her arm.

"Here you are, Ifanwy and Owen." I smiled and spoke in Welsh. When I am moved or alone I use this language of the poets.

"Your loving grand-daughter as brave as any saint, as brave as St Alban himself, is our newest and youngest abbess."

Then she ran to them, embraced and kissed them. My heart is in my mouth and eyes. I am in the presence of a half-starved young woman who knows no fear. She treats the whitening disease with disdain and dismissal as if it had no importance, as if she herself had the protection of Jesus and the Mary who washed his feet. Such a faith and love. For the moment I am quite overwhelmed and can say nothing. I have to turn away to hide the rush of moisture into and from my eyes. What is their temple – a derelict eeler's hut wrecked by gales, winter and flood and yet it is a holy place, as holy as any church in Christendom. I am a poor specimen in comparison – she could ask me if she wished, just as Diogenes said to Alexander the Great, to move out of her light. But she is more modest than the philosopher.

Only two hours before I stood in terror and mortal dread of lepers; now I have ordained a young woman to look after them, and other outcasts. My shadow does not reach her. I stand three paces back, no longer from fear, but because the old man and his wife are embarrassed and ashamed of their hands and the mud-rags which bind their foot sores. Yet for them, this is the first time since their banishment that they have become again two persons, ordinary travellers, albeit with a horrifying illness, no longer the carriers of demons and the evil eye.

"Listen carefully." I spoke gently. "There has been a vile and monstrous crime against John the Old Saxon at his monastery on the Isle of Athelney. But God, in His mercy, has sent to us ..." I spread my hands towards my friend the Coptic surgeon, "...Sister Emma. With her great knowledge of healing she has restored his life to him." They are listening closely. I apologize to Emma for she has no idea what I'm saying, but we have a long ride home – there is much time to explain. "The monks of Athelney had some of their brothers domiciled in an outreach house, you may have seen it, an old Roman farmhouse between Langport and the Abbey at Muchelney. Now the building is empty, the recalled monks await their punishment and many will be returned to France."

I look at Alwyn. "Do you know this place, Sister Alwyn? Have you passed by that way?"

She doesn't look to me but to Owen, the grandfather, as if they shared some incident concerning the place – alms ... or dogs.

"We know it, Bishop Asser." See how this girl grows in stature minute by minute. "The monks gave us nothing, only their dogs."

Yes, I had expected that. "I'm sorry. Two of those monks who set their dogs on you are evil criminals. They attacked their abbot in front of his altar. I am to judge them soon. In a trial."

They listen and nod. They are intelligent and must know as well as I do that under Alfred's laws there are three death penalties – for treason, for assaulting the King and for attacking a priest in a church. "One of these men is still almost only a child. Too young for death. Pray for me."

Alwyn now does look at me, a troubled and steady gaze. "We shall be praying for you, Bishop Asser."

"Thank you."

A young woman and two lepers will pray for their bishop. God is present.

"I want the three of you to make your way to the old Roman farm at Midelney. Take the marsh paths."

She is still gazing at me; it is unsettling. It contains a rare light, an intensity of insight and emotion.

"Yes, my Lord Bishop. We shall go there. All the paths and tracks are known to us. We leave at once." This grand-daughter is now an abbess – no longer the starved young woman with her bones outlining her face, arms and limbs. She must surely be the first and only barefoot abbess in the whole of Wessex. And beyond. I nodded.

"Good. Take possession of the old Roman barn. Make a home for your grand-parents in the wash-house, it is but a small distance away from the main building. It is large and there is space enough for a hospice ... for other lepers."

"God is merciful, Bishop Asser. You are his merciful vicar."

How does she know these words and feelings. Was she born a saint?

"Thank you. I shall name our new House after your Order of Carmel – The Garden House of God and St Christopher ..."

I paused to think.

"The trial is next week. There may be time – I shall make time – to bring you over some of the things you'll need. We shall come with several pack-horses. And later, when you have settled in, I should like you to receive Sister Emma. She can no longer stay where she is."

I traced a cross over them. "Go in peace with the love of God and His Son Jesus Christ ... *In nomine Patris, Filius et Spiritus Sanctus.*"

We went our separate ways. Such a change has fallen upon them, bewildering, but I have no fear; the thought of their new lives uplifts me. As we set out on our homeward journey Sister Emma said, "You are a wise, brave and kind man, Asser."

"Thank you. Yet I was none of those things a few hours ago. You are leading me, Sister Emma, into an enlightenment." And I had this thought as we left behind my new abbess and her kin with their sickness as frightening as any on the earth – 'how will King Alfred accept a leper hospice in the Sedge Moor, no more than a day's walk from the Houses at Muchelney and Athelney ... and what will he say to them being children of Carmel?'

There it is, laid before you all as it happened. Back to today. Time has passed. A week. And we are returning with one heavily laden packhorse. Emma is close behind. I should like to tell her about the Roman farmhouse at Midelney. As the track is wider and less slippery, I bring her up to me, alongside. The history is like so many of these farms and villas now almost lost forever.

"The old Roman barn, I think you should know its history, the more so as you will be living there soon. The Romans were remarkable people, so advanced in building, law and civil works baths, even hot pipes beneath the floors to warm their villas. We are fortunate indeed they came to us and stayed for 400 years, leaving a culture behind that will never die out. This area, the Levels, they set about draining as they did elsewhere in their Britannia ... in the East. Here they wanted fertile land for the veterans of the Second Augusta. And some chose to live here – perhaps they were farmers before, or their parents and knew the marshes around Rome."

She said nothing but listened, sometimes touching the neck of her horse, sometimes turning behind to encourage the one behind.

"Sending unruly monks here was a divisive and dubious practice from the outset ... and I share some of the blame – I saw and heard the mutterings and whispers but did nothing about it. I had a reluctance to interfere, John was a man I respected and admired, a leader of reflective and holy men, but not a master of embittered Franks. He is a man of spirituality; he doesn't have the sharpness and manner to deal with disobedient monks. How could they love and respect a Saxon Abbot placed over them. Wasn't there a crime set in motion, and waiting to happen? Don't I bear half the blame? How can I, tomorrow, ask for the death penalty, Emma?"

"Tomorrow, Asser, you will know what to do."

"Thank you ... I shall pray for guidance."

We can see the great barn now. It looms large, grey and silent. I can see already that many of the roof tiles are off and as we watch birds are flying in and out.

"It's in poor shape, Emma. I shall need a tiler – and the man I find will have a job forever more. But look closely and you can see something hopeful – some of the windows still have their glass in them. And there's a problem – in England we've almost lost the art of glass making." I smile and shrug.

"We may have to send to Aquitaine for a glazier. Let's move closer."

We were met at the wattle fence in the lychgate, by our new abbess. Today she has left behind her marsh rags and wears a clean white surplice drawn in at the waist with a sash. A shaft of midday sunlight reflects up at us from the mother-of-pearl cross I placed around her neck last week. Emma jumps from her horse, runs over and embraces her. The warmth between them moves me – already they are friends.

I dismount onto the gate bench – rather staid and bishoply. I am excited.

What a fine and gracious barn, as high as our church at Aller. I admire its strong Roman walls and the way in which tiles have been inserted. The Romans left a lot behind when they withdrew from these islands, but they took much more with them.

"Father Bishop ..." I like that address, it is warm and affectionate and the right way for a young woman abbess to address her Vicar-in-Christ.

"Yes, Alwyn?" I smiled. "Are you going to show us how you've changed things for the better?"

We tether the horses to a rail. Emma is concerned for them and hurries in for water ... and she found some hay. The monks, it seemed, did do some work after all. First I'm taken inside, and yes, it is already far different from when the Franks slept here – no longer does it reek of urine. The Welsh family have been working hard to bring back a freshness from the past when it was a vast hay and wheat barn for the district and the outlying colonia. In a single week they've cleared up the detritus of years of carelessness, savagery, dirt and disrespect. The fresh air that has been brought in holds within it scents of spring and a sweetish pungency; it is coming from the rushes and herbs they had spread across the floor. The sun too is playing its part – it enters from the intact west window and is full of promise, the promise of better days to come, and summer when all England rediscovers its inherent beauty.

I exclaim, "Why Alwyn... just look at all this! How much better you have made it! You have brought in a natural holiness."

She is happy now – her diffidence is being shed day by day. "We cleaned and washed it all down, Father Bishop."

In places the old Roman mosaic showed through the reed matting, so lovely in its vivid colouring, a brightness of design as though the tesserae had only been laid yesterday. At the east end under the morning window, they had erected a cross with burning candles on either side. There were no visible signs of this space having been slept in by any of the family and the interior has now the feeling of a holy and sacred place. We have now a spiritual home for Carmelite nuns and a hospice for lepers where their sickness can be helped and where they will no longer be objects of fear and disgust.

I pointed, "I shall have those other windows sealed for you by next winter – no more rain, hail, snow and birds will be able to force their way into our new abbey. And with God's help, and the help of others you will maintain this place for years to come. Thank you. We shall try and get all the building work done this coming summer, Alwyn. Until then – try and keep warm. This hall is not habitable as it is. King Alfred will be impressed ... though the presence of a leper hospice may take longer for him to accept. Yet he is the kindest and wisest of men."

We move on and are taken by Alwyn to the outhouses, the washrooms, to see what is happening there, and how the grandparents are settling in. It is to my discredit – a weakness – that I still have some fear and nervousness. My heart is beating more quickly. A man of little courage, yet I have at this moment leading me a remarkable saintly girl of only 16 years. My fast heartbeat is shameful.

I shall describe these building in a little detail so that an image of this new-found hospice remains in the mind's-eye. There are three buildings close together, one with a chimney. All three are low-built and have intact roofing of terracotta tiles, not raided and stolen, for this place is virtually unknown, hidden within the marsh. And unlike those on the great barn, they had not been lifted off by storms or frosts, why I can't be sure – perhaps it is because they are lower and more out of the wind, tighter bound and cover a much less wide space. Originally these were the baths and remain much as the Romans left them though the boiler and hypocaust have long since disappeared.

For all that, I believe we have become a kinder people and no longer derive pleasure from violence – the circus and gladiators. And slavery is vanishing from these islands.

Owen and Ifanwy were standing outside but withdrew as we approached to maintain a distance. I raised my hand in a greeting, traced a blessing and looked to the two women beside me.

"How are they? Do they feel better ..." I shaped the outline of the building with my left hand, "... in there? Is it dry and warm? Can they sleep and settle into such a change?"

I can see fresh bandages showing at the tops of some soft boots.

Emma answered. "They are much better, Asser. The sores on their hands and feet are healing." She touched the arm of the young woman at her side. "I have given my balm to Alwyn and she is rubbing it in twice a day."

The look that passed between them was light-hearted and half-smiling – they have become as if sisters. But what I hear astonishes me.

"What! You rub balm into a leper's sore!" I look from one to the other. The Coptic woman is not in any way dismayed.

"Yes. Asser. We rub in the ointments. I have done it often, the sores will heal. I have used them many times before, in Rosetta, to a hundred people, not just two. The sores are not the disease, only injuries to skin where there is no longer any feeling, and there is no warning of sharp stones, or heat ... or if they are wet, or parched."

Scales are falling from my eyes. Feelings of disgust and fear are being replaced by facts. I am astonished. It is so simple. There is only fear and loathing when such logic and observations are unknown. I call to the old woman. "What good work you've been doing here, Ifanwy." Welsh words, softer than those in English.

Still she puts her hands behind her though they are now enclosed in a kind of glove.

"We wish to thank you, Lord Bishop Asser, for all your kindness and help to us. You are a blessing sent by God."

"Were it so. But thank you. Each of us is loved in His sight. Tell me, what tasks you and Owen have been doing."

"Cleaning, Lord Bishop. The men here were not Welsh monks. We do not have such uncouth people."

Aren't those words a miracle in themselves – a dignity restored? Only last week they were felt to be the most unclean objects in the entire kingdom.

"Good. I am pleased. And next?"

Her husband answered me. "We shall be in the gardens. They are a wilderness, and a waste."

The two left us to begin work there and I went inside looking at everything and noting what was needed to the walls, windows and doors. Outside I was led through to a walled garden where already the old couple were at work digging and throwing aside tall weeds, a gardener and his wife, no longer only rejected objects banished to the shunned world of lepers. And I could hear singing, softly, a Welsh song that my mother had taught me and was played by harpers at gatherings, 'Cym brae'. Is it from the woman or from both? I am very moved.

"They are right, Asser. You possess the compassion of Christ."

Tears spring to my eyes. I am seeing strength arising from the weak. Just as it was said.

"Thank you, Emma. But I still have a long way to go. You are a guide to knowledge, and knowledge is the handmaiden to compassion. Let's unload the horse and bring in our gifts for this new hospice of light, and healing."

On our return I was lost in thought. Tomorrow is the day set for the trial of the two Franks. I shall be called upon to be the judge of it all, a Solomon ... and how shall I manage that. So much about those events disturb me and have snatched away my sleep. I shall get though only with God's help, His presence ... may I find and use the compassion they say I have. I cannot order the death of two of God's souls. It is not in my nature, nor in my Christian faith.

ELEVEN

Trial

I have now rejected the dining room for this criminal hearing; it is too cold and too disruptive for the brothers. Instead I have converted my own rooms, such that they now appear as a diocesan court, making the two spaces into one by removing my sleeping screen and bedroll. The bed itself has been pushed back against the wall, covered with a linen drape and along the edge facing into the room I have placed law books – Codices of Roman Law and our own case law of Wessex, judgments and revisions by Alfred himself. It is a reminder of the rarity of such an event as this – criminality within the church is almost unknown, yet it does happen. Monks, priest and nuns are not given to violence, drunkenness and immorality.

I have placed from the refectory a broad table and set behind it a bench with a woolsack and red cover. Yet we are overshadowed by black, the colour of death. I have ordered that no black shall be displayed, instead Sebastian has set the standards of King Alfred and pennants for the Houses of Cerdic, Canterbury, Winchester and Sherborne. The table itself is covered with a lesser pallium and draped across it a lace from our Glastonbury weavers containing two Christian symbols, the Chi-Ro delicately embroidered in coloured threads, and the fish motifs.

Normally in simpler cases – theft discipline and disputes, I sit alone. Today is different. Quite another matter. As serious an offence as it is possible to be. I shall have Sebastian on my left, a lay wing-member, and to my right the court recorder, Emma. You may say that in fact and appearance we are the tribunal of old – and there is some truth in that, but we are not equally empowered like then. Only the presiding bishop, the chairman, pronounces judgment, though he may consult and take advice from his side members. Nor has the Crown powers to set aside the decisions arrived at unless it is deemed to be treasonable and injurious to the king.

All precepts devolve finally from Alfred. He has rewritten, reshaped all the formal law books coming down to us from Justinian and his forebear King Ine. In Courts Episcopal, the mandate is wide, decisions final and binding – but there are set boundaries. The court has no jurisdiction beyond that of the church and offences committed in its name or within its houses. We are not a court of doctrine, nor may we pronounce on land matters, ownership and boundaries, foundations or disestablishment. It is not a court of appeal against edicts from Rome. As for punishment – the penance, manner and length of convictions, penalties levied on supporting kin and to injured parties, we tread carefully so as not to trespass on civil procedures. Our ways and thoughts you will witness as this trial unfolds – as it is about to do. The two criminals, for that is what they are, have no claim to innocence, absence, or mistakes of identity. They have been named by John Saxon himself and their faces confirmed by the chapel sacristan.

We are assembled. The hearing is public.

Some brothers are seated – the older ones – and others stand around the wall. The two would-be murderers are present. Without chains. Their two warders stand close on either side – strong English countrymen who will brook no nonsense of any kind. Upon my table are two black caps. It is required by law and precedence, though I find their presence disturbing and distasteful marking up the gravity of the proceedings and a sentence that may pronounce they shall be hanged. I have already said in these pages that I do not incline to capital punishment. It is the bedrock of Christian belief and teaching that each and every soul is treasured and of singular value to The Almighty Father – repentance of the sinner is to be embraced, as Christ has told us so many times. Nor shall I order them to be tortured. What penance I lay upon them shall be severe but not wantonly cruel. A Bishop of Wessex in Alfred's kingdom and led by The Son cannot and will not call out the whip-masters. Do we not all walk in frailty? Is not each one of us capable of falling from Grace?

I shall here open the common roll as it is currently laid out, but shall not comment on the new and as yet untried borough Courts.

Broadly speaking – an offender is first brought before a District Court where the case is heard by a Court Reeve. And remember this, court reeves are not the rag-bag of clerks they were. Alfred has put a stop to ignorant and arbitrary decisions. He has stamped out malfeasance, that is to say all the past bribery, threats from family members and judgments based on stupidity and bias. Now lawyers are educated men, readers, and mostly thegns. Alfred will punish any man who hands down a bad, ill-considered decision. The reeve will find himself reprimanded, suspended and sent for further education and training.

A district court is not censorious but corrective of wrong-doing, minor crimes, disputes over property and land, theft and the receiving of stolen goods. The reeve will determine the fine to be served on the guilty party or upon his family. Also the level of penance meted out. And that is what I do for crimes within my compass – blasphemy, oath-breaking and all church misdemeanours and corruptions. Let us leave other details to those who wish to delve. I shall touch upon the appeal mechanisms, which will not apply today. Alfred will sit and if an appeal is considered due for one reason or another – he will rule as the final arbiter.

We are ready. I nod to my clerk. "Brother Stephen ... bring the court to order, please. We are ready to begin hearing the charges."

I turn to my pupil. "You may question these two when you wish, Sebastian. I shall be glad of your wisdom and insights." He looks at me with a curious expression as if he suspects me of mocking. Yet deep down he knows that I do value his common sense, his common touch.

"I know about horses, Asser, not murderous monks."

I touch his arm. "Of course. And that's why you've been asked to sit with us."

Emma is still within her vow of silence. She has opened in front of her the court ledger for recording the morning's proceedings – the names, oath-helpers, the evidence and the outcome. I smile at her. She has at hand several sharpened quills and a flask of her own ink.

"Are you ready, Sister Emma?"

She nods and places beneath her book and inks a linen sheet to protect the delicate Glastonbury embroidery covering the table. I find that so thoughtful and admire her carefulness. The prisoners, after being shown to us, have been removed to an ante-room. My door is rapped three times with the moot-rod and the monks are led back in by Brother Stephen – each man held firmly in the grip of his warder, the young one after the older one. Precedence is not just in court matters, it has invaded everywhere; the church itself is far from exempt. Behind the two comes John Saxon followed by Aethelwold, his chapel sacristan. Finally at a little distance comes Alfred's representative, his daughter Aethelgifu, *in loco regis*. I have permitted entry of the remaining Athelney monks, those who have not been sent back to France.

I stand and open the day's business with a prayer, asking Almighty God to lay upon us His wisdom and guidance in judgment – His mercy.

"You may all sit, except the prisoners. Unhand them."

The attackers looked dishevelled, distraught and downcast, as well they might. By this evening they may be hanged from the Hanging Ash on Ham Hill. I take the two black caps from the table and pass them to Stephen my clerk. There is a profound sighing. A murmuring. There will be no deaths after all. The younger prisoner rocks on his feet at that revelation, stumbles and I thought he was going to faint. I told his warder to hold him once more. I addressed the older Frank who led this savage attack.

"You … are you Oswald, monk of Athelney, also known as Esquith, formerly of the house at Midelney?" He is swarthy, dirty and unshaven. Red-eyed. I hear hardness in his voice and disrespect.

"I am Oswald, Lord Bishop." Such defiance. He is not yet repentant. I turn to his younger companion.

"Tell the court your name."

"Amatus, Lord Bishop." His voice is the very opposite – tremulous and weak. He is less to blame than the villain who led the sword attack, and his name bears witness that he was once a child much loved.

"Where were you born, Amatus?"

"At Nîmes, My Lord."

"How long have you been a monk?"

"Seven years, sir."

"And where was your induction and tonsure?"

"At Alès, My Lord. In the Abbey church of Saint Jean."

"How old were you then?"

"Fourteen, sir."

"And how old were you when you came to England?"

"I have been here three years, sir. I am twenty-one."

I looked away. So young – to be taken at fourteen from his family and then brought out from his own country to serve God in England – an alien, cold and frightening place. Yet ... was I not the same age as this unfortunate when I entered God's service as a novice in training. I was luckier – at home and under the tender gaze of my uncle. I cannot and shall not bring down the full weight of Alfred's Law Book upon this foolish and unhappy boy's head.

"You have brought disgrace. Amatus, onto your mother and father who placed you in the Church's care and protection for a life dedicated to Jesus Christ, his teachings and to walk in the paths of righteousness. You have brought disgrace upon your city of Nîmes and upon the abbey church where you were granted acceptance into a holy life by priests who saw in you someone they could teach and trust. It is a sorry and wretched business. How do you plead?"

"Guilty. My Lord Asser. I am ashamed and deeply penitent ... so ashamed."

I turned to the older man. A monk with cold and embittered eyes. "Oswald, how do you plead?"

"Guilty."

The man invites a whipping and the hangman's rope – an old trouble-maker full of anger, pride and conceit. I motioned the court clerk to come forward.

"Bring before us Abbot John Saxon and his chapel sacristan Aethelwold."

From the back of the courtroom he brought out my friend, colleague and fellow tutor to the Royal House. He has a limp. Around his neck is bound a white silken sash covering the raw scars beneath.

"Brother Abbot, please tell the court your name, and for my recorder."

"I am John Saxon, My Lord Bishop. Abbot of Athelney."

His sacristan is quite different in build – tall, lean and with the forward stoop adopted by very tall men. I asked him to identify himself.

"I am Aethelwold, Bishop Asser, chapel priest and sacristan to my abbot."

"Thank you." I returned my gaze to the former. "John of Saxony, do you see standing before you in this court the two monks who attacked you in your chapel and who nearly cut your life from you?"

He pointed, his voice thick with emotion. "There! They are the ones!"

Yet beneath the roughness of his voice is a spiritual man who at times wears the quiet and gentleness of a child. I pressed him further.

"Oswald and Amatus ... they are the ones who attacked you?"

"Yes."

"Thank you. You may go back to where you were sitting. I may call upon you again." I then turned to the chapel priest.

"Brother Aethelwold, are these the two men who attacked and attempted to murder your abbot? On the 28th day of February, a Friday, the second Ember Day in Lent ... in the morning?"

"Yes, my Lord Bishop."

"Then tell us in your own words what you saw. Only that. What took place. Nothing else. And please take your time."

Aethelwold raised his hand and pointed at the old monk. "Brother Oswald rushed into the chapel while my Abbot John was kneeling and praying before the altar." His voice shook as he relived the terrible moment.

"Go on."

"I was in the aisle making preparations for our own prayers in the second mattin that follows our daybreak Mass." His voice was beginning to rise.

"Could you see well in the morning light?"

"Oh yes ... it was shocking and terrifying – these two monks from

Midelney rushing in shouting and screaming. They set about Abbot John with their swords."

"I understand there was only one sword."

The good man was silenced. He paled. "I'm sorry, My Lord. Only one sword."

"You must be accurate with your evidence, Aethelwold. This vile and evil assault carries with it the death penalty. You are giving evidence on oath. Your words might hang a man."

"I am very sorry. I was reliving the attack and the screams, and all the blood. The horror of it all."

"Continue but be precise. You may be questioned by the oath-helpers and made to look stupid. You are the main witness. Carry on with what you heard and saw."

He then straightened up and I could see what a tall, towering man he is. He carries on more slowly, voice more assured.

"As I remember it, Brother Oswald ran in with his sword, shouting loudly ... and was followed by Brother Amatus."

"How can it be 'his sword'? Does a brother of a religious monastic house own a sword?"

"I mean the sword he was carrying, Bishop Asser."

"Very good. And did the other brother have a sword?"

"No, sir."

I turned to the court clerk who had taken up a position beside Sister Emma, behind her chair.

"Usher ... bring forward the sword, please."

The weapon was brought and laid flat on the table in front of me – a Roman short-sword. I looked at it for some time, picked it up and turned it over. Blood marks still stained the blade. I passed it to Sebastian to examine and return to the sacristan.

"Where was this sword found?"

"Outside the chapel, My Lord ... where it was thrown."

"And is this the one you saw Oswald strike John Saxon with?"

"Yes, sir."

"How do you know?"

"Because it is short, unlike the swords of today."

"Thank you. You may return to your place." I looked at Sebastian. There is a similarity between Sebastian and the man leaving us. Both are tall, thin and quick.

"You may question the two prisoners before us."

To my surprise he immediately recalled Aethelwold. The sacristan was disconcerted and put out. He must have thought his evidence giving was over and he was far from pleased to be questioned for a second time by a lesser brother. I saw tension and irritation in his eyes. My assistant began.

"Brother Aethelwold. These two men ... what do you know about them?"

"They are Frankish monks brought over by King Alfred."

"Why should they attack your abbot ... what was the reason?"

"They are full of bitterness. Every time they come back to us they are insolent and stir up the others."

"About what?"

"Being here. Away from their people and having to live in a separate house some distance from us, at Midelney. They regard that as a punishment."

"And is it?"

The sacristan made no answer but gave a slight shrug and looked down the court to find the eyes of John Saxon. I intervened sharply.

"Do not look around you, Brother Aethelwold. Answer the question put to you ... is it a punishment?"

"How can I answer that? I do not set punishments, My Lord."

"Don't be clever with me. This is a court trying two would-be assassins and the penalty is death. Answer the question and remain respectful. Are some of the monks of Athelney placed over at Midelney because you don't want them living with you?"

"Yes, my Lord Bishop."

"We will strike your previous answer from the records. Continue."

It is a curious feature of the man that he loses his stoop when annoyed. Sebastian let him go back to his place for the second time then indicated to our clerk that he now wanted Oswald to be brought to the oath-boards.

"Brother Oswald, where did you get that sword from?"

He raised it up. My assistant and pupil has talents I have not been aware of. The man before us is uncouth in every way – no sorrow, no repentance. It is as the sacristan said – a monk full of insolence and bitterness. I am glad Sebastian has taken up the examination.

"I dug it up. In the vegetable garden."

"When was that."

"A month ago."

"You cleaned it up and polished it?"

"Yes."

Sebastian eased his finger along the blade edge. "And sharpened it."

The old man looked down for the first time – sullen and wary. A man quite unsuited to a spiritual calling. "Yes."

"Yes, what?"

"I sharpened it."

It was a significant moment. The court knew it. Why would a monk sharpen a sword he had found if not with evil intent. My rising assistant has gifts for a courtroom, as an inquisitor. I have made the right choice to prepare him for high office. Sebastian lays down the sword but so places it that the tip points at Brother Oswald.

"Tell us. Tell the court why you kept this sword to yourself, cleaned it and polished it ... and sharpened it."

Suddenly all the pent-up anger in the old monk burst out. He swung around and jabbed a shaking finger towards John Saxon "Because I wanted to kill him!"

It sounded savage. Murderous. The ferocity of the outburst shocked the court. A stunned and profound silence, an in-drawing of breath. Sebastian impresses me more and more – maintaining a calm and incisive voice, distancing himself from the man's rage.

"You planned this attack in cold blood, waiting your chance. This was not the violence of sudden heat."

The Frank was doomed, but I let it continue for at that moment I saw a change in him – head and eyes low, voice reduced to a whisper.

"Yes. I waited."

"What need had you of a young innocent brother like Amatus for your wickedness?"

"I cannot run. The abbot might have run away from me."

I turned to Emma. "Record that firmly, please ... it is of much significance." I nodded to Sebastian that he might continue his questioning.

"Brother Oswald ... why did you want to kill your abbot, John of Saxony?"

The heat in the man surged back up – he would have spat anywhere else.

"Because he is a Saxon pig who keeps us in a cold, filthy place and has dragged us from our homes into a god-forsaken wetland, a stinking marsh unfit for any man ... save lepers."

He is now waving his hands and arms about. "I have every reason to be in a rage ... and I'm not sorry. We were banished, not allowed to live in Athelney with our own kind, our friends and brothers-in-Christ. Banished to a disgusting ruin filled with flies, fever, fogs and filth!"

Such oratory and rhetoric. There is more to Brother Oswald than I first thought, he is now shouting and waving his fist at us all. "Hang me if you want to, I don't care. My life is finished. It ended when I left France." He sank to his knees, all anger broken. "My land! My country! Oh my people!"

He covered his face with his hands and broke down into sobbing, choking and coughing. Pitiful, and harrowing. More animal than human. I must bring all this to a close. I wait until it lessens then call his warders to raise him up and face us once more. Blame is not mitigated, but no man can witness all this without asking how and why ... and feel some compassion. Alfred brings over his Frankish monks to fill a monastery he alone wants. The abbot he appoints is a gentle scholar incapable of coping with their resentment. The bishop – myself – takes no action to grasp and siphon off the poison building more and more, month on month. I made no attempt to open this box of vipers before one reared up and struck, as it must. I sighed deeply. My heart is troubled.

"Bring forward the oath-helpers."

My clerk shakes his head. "There are none, My Lord."

"Very well. We have heard enough." I look from Oswald to Amatus, then back to the old man again. "Do you confess your guilt, deny nothing and yet still throw yourselves at us unrepentant?" There is a sharpness entering my voice. It is a horrific business from start to finish. Sister Emma raises her head and sets her quill into the ink-flask. She writes a note for me. 'The younger brother Amatus is ashamed and repentant, Asser.' She is right. I shall punish them separately.

"Come forward, Oswald." I wave the old Frank to me with his warder close by.

"Lower your head. Kneel. You are deep in sin." I motion the warders to take some paces back.

"Oswald, you are guilty of supreme wickedness and deserve to be bound, lashed, tortured and hanged. That is the Law and the penalty for your evil-doing. But none of these I shall order because you acted out of rage, and bitterness – not malice for gain or fornication. Your attack was an act of murder. Upon you I shall set a punishment to fit your crime." The man gives a sigh from his soul as if welcoming the end. "A death sentence ... but suspended." The court is riveted. A deep foreboding silence hangs over it like an incoming storm. My recorder looks up at me, eyebrows raised. A suspended death sentence defies her imagination. I nod and tense my lips.

"Oswald. Raise your head and look at me. And listen." He does so. But his gaze is inward. "You shall be stripped of all holy orders and become a slave to spend the rest of your life among lepers." Now he really does look. With utter astonishment.

"Amongst lepers, My Lord Bishop? Am I to be placed with lepers?"

"So far there are only two – my countrymen. You will care for them as if they were your own kin – fetch and carry water, clean and change their dressings ..." His face is full of wonder. To him this is a miracle. He shakes his head. Dumbfounded.

"Where is this place, Holy Father?"

"Your house at Midelney has been cleaned and purified. The outlying buildings are now a leper hospice. I bind you to it. Should you try to escape you will be hunted down by hounds and torn apart."

There is a whispering around us, as if the first rains had arrived. Many would prefer to be hanged than to be bonded to lepers as their servant to care, nurse and cook for. But not this man. There is courage behind his bitterness. I point "Return to your place. Amatus ... come forward."

The young man comes forward on his own. His warders have released him. He is in fear and trembling. I am not a cruel man. It disturbs me to see his abject manner and terror.

"Kneel and lower your head. You have walked in darkness and in great sin." He kneels and covers his head with his arms. "Brother Amatus – Almighty God and our Saviour Lord Jesus Christ chose you to be a disciple and you have repaid them by acting like a Judas. But you are young, stupid and easily led. However, I see you are full of sorrow and repent of your evil crime – and your good Abbot John of Saxony lives. He has been healed by Christ and by the hands of Sister Emma. I am returning you to the novitiate for five years, then you may ask to be reinstated as an ordinand for tonsure."

He brings his hands together in prayer. No sinner was more penitent than this young Absolom.

"Amatus ... I am binding you to the house at Midelney for five years. But it has changed. Take off your shoes." For the first time he gazes at me in surprise. He crouches awkwardly and unwinds the cords from his ankles and removes his sandals. Then he stands holding them out in front of him as if they were some kind of sacrificial offering. Does he believe I shall now whip his soles as they do in Hispania?

"Amatus ... you will assist the Abbess Alwyn in her new Carmelite foundation and shall remain barefoot for five winters and five summers. You will help her in all things – like you she is young, a woman who has suffered much. You will be to her as an older brother, do everything she asks of you and more besides. You will sleep in the robing room behind the vestry and protect the convent night and day. If you are accused of fornication you will be hanged."

He bows his head, his young face full of tears. I say a silent prayer that I have acted wisely and with justice. Our Saviour sends down his love for us all, sinners and the righteous, heathen and Christian, onto the green lands of Wessex, upon its willows and on its weeds. Blessed is the Name of the Lord. I call the wardens to me.

"Take these convicts back down to the cells but do not reset their chains. Bring them hot soup and bread, rub lavender oil into their chain-bruises. They have sinned deeply and have been punished for it. Tomorrow Sebastian will conduct them to the Carmelite Abbess. The court rises."

Stephen, our court clerk, repeats it in a loud voice … "The court rises."

We, the tribunal, are the first to leave.

TWELVE

Mons acutus ... Montacute

How curious things are – tomorrow is a saint's day ... for the Egyptian Father St Anaestasius, Bishop of Alexandria. So many matters Egyptian have been entering my life in these last three months. My friend, our Coptic physician from Rosetta, Antioch and Padua performed another surgical miracle last week, which I shall set down in this record after we have returned from today's expedition. It is Wednesday. We are in the fifth week after Easter and it is the day of St James and St Philip. I am answering a summons, a Royal Command, to present myself to Alfred. He has sent to me his thegn and message bearer, Edmund Swift. It seems I am to be called to account.

I have sent this regal Apollo back and shall leave when I'm ready. In the meantime there are some entries to make into this little volume of jottings – my diary.

The call to Montacute, as it is now known, concerns, as you may have guessed, the trial and punishment of the two Franks. And there is more. Alfred is showing curiosity towards my Sister Emma. He is tormented by the bitterness in his bowels and is desperate for help, for an easing. The pills and potions sent over from Jerusalem, from the Patriarch Alias, have been useless. They have neither cured, relieved nor reduced the fire in his evacuations. As for the trial, his daughter Aethelgifu will have handed him her report – the procedure, indictment and outcome ... and about the lepers. The banishment of the two Franks to them. She will have told him I did not bring down the full weight of her father's codex.

I shall set out after breakfast. I should not want to travel in this weather without the warmth of honey-gruel inside me. We shall be going to the fortress and Montacute, one of our newer defences and built without the need of forced labour Alfred had to use to build the one at Athelney. He is a severe taskmaster when the mood takes him. He never rests. We have had a spate of new forts in case the Danes come back, or the barbaric Norsemen with their burnings, plunder and cruelties. It is little wonder that the Romans called them as from Ultima Thule – the end of everything, and had no intention of venturing up there through their ice-forests and frozen seas. Praise be to God they haven't come south – yet. There was a time when we valued horsemanship in battle. Now it is almost forgotten and one day we shall pay heavily for that neglect. In Normandy it has become a finely honed system – swift cavalry and sharp-eyed archers.

Montacute, like so many of our defensive sites here in Wessex, is a Roman foundation. They were superb builders with skilled architects, and they understood the secrets of cement. So many of these modern methods they took away with them despite our pleas. And what folly afterwards – we invited in the Saxon mercenaries. All deep in the past now. Our own Saxon origins are blended in, as were the Romans – it was only in Wales that the British survived … and in the outposts of Cornwall. Be that as it may – our invaders now are raw, uncivilised and uncouth. I thank God each day for the gift of King Alfred carrying forward a different and more delicate banner, and for the loyalty of our fighting men.

As for Montacute, the lands at the foot of the upthrust have been granted to the Benedictines of Cluny for their priory. Much is happening there. Pax Romana is for the moment being held and religious houses are founded – our abbey. The New Minster is uprising in Winchester. The fort we are visiting is said to have been built over the ruins of a Roman temple, a shrine to the God of Light, a deity they borrowed from the Persian Empire. When the sun comes up in the eastern sky and spreads its light across Yeovil Marsh, the top of Mons Acutus is lit up with a rare radiance, and it is that which awed our Roman forebears, and why they built a temple there for votives to Mithram.

From Sherborne to Montacute is a nine-mile walk, easily done with a fresh start. Sebastian is coming along, restraining himself to my pace, though if I sent him ahead he would run. He is a born athlete. We are well into our task now and he's talkative this morning – about the trial, of course, and the lepers and the recent act of mercy and precision undertaken yesterday by our astonishing physician-surgeon. More about that later. He's a good companion and the time passes quickly – nor is it so cold as when we came this way last time.

As we approach we are greeted by a man on horseback – well dressed and impressive – the king's reeve. He is not one of the serving men from Alfred's standing war-band but a uniformed soldier-scholar based at Langport. Alfred maintains a sparse court. He has a pattern, a regime, for the standing army, no more the summoning of the fyrd from fields and forges. At any one time half his thegns are in military service while the remainder carry on with their kin and daily work. After a fixed period the first half is stood down and the others take their place. In this way the war-band is continually manned and is ready for any surprise attack. Our welcoming reeve dismounts and greets us warmly. I recognise him – he was at the baptism in Aller when our world was shaken and invaded by the rattles and drums of our Welsh lepers.

At the stockade entrance, Sebastian is allowed to go down and meet the Cluniac brothers who are marking out the foundations of their new priory. I am taken up past the six men-at-arms, Alfred's praetorian guards and into the king's living quarters. He is lying on a bed, face taut with pain. Ah, if only it was within my power to release him from these daily torments and suffering. He is alone. His wife doesn't travel with a moving court anymore. It is no longer appropriate, and perhaps she finds him poor company with his daytime anguish and night fears. Besides, she has given him five children and for certain prefers the company of her daughter and women friends. Who could blame her for that? She is a loyal and good wife, and what is there up here for her to do? Nor could she lighten the pains from his bowels. No one can. No physician has ever helped him. Only God. Thirty years ago in Cornwall Alfred prayed to be released from the torments of the flesh and the itch. He was helped, but there came in another affliction – much worse.

My king is pale and downcast, doesn't sit up to greet me but holds his head in his right hand like a man in the throes of some piercing toothache. With the other hand he gestures a restrained and distancing welcome. He is in a mood – sadness, despair and pain. Yet his eyes are brightening.

"Asser! How good to see you – come and sit beside me like you used to. I find it too quiet and oppressive here."

"You don't have your sons with you ... Edward?"

"Away. Always away. The Danes ... what a scourge they are! And like starving wolves, never satisfied."

"Guthrum?"

"What do they care for him now ... a peacemaker and a Christian. How can he tame packs of wild dogs?" He sighed, took his hand from his cheek and sat up. "I miss you, Asser. Why do you stay away? We had happy days, didn't we? Sit down here and help me. Lift me from this cold and greyness in my soul."

I do as he asks. The serving-men are waved away. I leave him for a moment to go to the window and tie back the screens to let in some life-giving daylight, to let in the first airs of a new season, a touch of summer days to come – the sun's blessings. When I am back at his side he waves a finger at me and admonishes me like a school-master.

"My friend, my daughter tells me you are behaving like a lunatic!"

I smile – his moods are like the sea-tide rising and falling, swirling and then submerging him. I shook my head wryly. "The moon is still new, Alfred, a crescent like they admire in Cordova." I spread my hands. "Where scholars and astronomers live. Not moon affected ... they are wise."

"Well then – was it wise, Asser, to send a murderer to be among lepers?"

"Why not? What a waste of good hands and feet to have them dangling from a rope."

"Listen my friend, do I want a colony of lepers so close to my convent at Muchelney ... so close to Athelney? And but a few miles walk from my borough at Langport?"

Both questions I have been expecting, thought about, but have no ready answers rehearsed.

"They are two simple, ordinary people. I do not call them lepers, only a man and his wife with their grand-daughter Alwyn – all from my country. Wales. The sores on their hands and feet are healing. The feet and fingers are numb like a limb in the snow, removed of all feeling. So they suffer burns because they do not know how hot fire is or how sharp a stone is under their foot … just as our own eelers get dead limbs from a winters marsh – frost bitten."

"So, my friend delivers me a lecture on a subject he knows nothing about. Asser, everyone fears lepers. They have their rattles and gongs, and have done so for a thousand years. Now my bishop believes he knows better than all of us. If it wasn't so amazing and you were not my friend and my children's tutor, I would be in a rage."

"I understand. I used to think like that, but it is as I say, Alfred. I have seen these things with my own eyes, touched the leper's grand-daughter. I have been taught by Sister Emma who has come to us from Egypt, and who has lived with and nursed them without coming to any harm. She has embraced them – and my old Welsh couple. She tells me she has seen that there are two kinds of this affliction – those who suffer in the face and are in mortal danger, and the others who have it in their hands and feet. The grand-daughter has been with them in their wanderings for three years, binding their wounds and taking the alms for their food. She is a saint, and untouched by it all."

"This child … does she not have it?"

"No."

He became quiet. His looks towards me from time to time are searching, yet I know that the gaze is more inward. He is searching himself. His tone has changed. Alfred is a man of exceptional gifts, and is compassionate.

"Are other lepers coming?"

"I hope so. We have the young woman to care for them. I have made her an abbess. She is a Carmelite."

"An abbess!" He shakes his head. "A girl … how old … sixteen? An abbess? Surely there is madness in your head. The follies of old age."

"Ah, but you haven't seen her, Alfred. Can you imagine it – at sixteen she asks leave to give up her calling and to be released from the convent to take over the care of her elderly kin. Is that not utterly remarkable in itself? Then she spends the next three years shunned by the entire world, living in dire poverty, hidden away – and yet there shines from her face such a light that she is the truest follower of Our Lord and Saviour I have ever met. If she were bishop and I her abbot it would not be unfitting."

The king lays back and closes his eyes. For many minutes he remained like that, withdrawing into a world inaccessible to me, breathing deeply. Suddenly he sat up. Eyes wide open.

"Tell me about this Egyptian physician, the woman who sat with you at the trial, your recorder, who is as silent as a German forest. My daughter knows her and brought her to you, but she tells me nothing. There is a vow? She has asked for manumission?"

"A vow of silence. You know she saved the life of John Asser by her Arabic skills."

He shrugged and spread his hands and fingers in a gesture of caution. "They are saying it is madness and magic. Asser, you are a man of God and a wise one – mostly – what is happening to you, my friend?"

How could I describe all the things I'd seen at Athelney on that day – the brazier, the incandescent rods burning the leaking flesh, the seamstress's stitches closing the gashes with a delicacy of a Glastonbury lace-woman. No one can understand who wasn't there to see it with their own eyes. Instead I said this.

"We have never before had such a surgeon and physician in Wessex. A disciple who learned her craft in Damascus and Padua, and in Rosetta where she cared for a hundred lepers … just like our Lord Jesus who did the same in the Holy Land among the sick, despised and excluded people. In the space of only a few months we have been blessed – two saints … one in a lifetime is more than most people might ever know. Almighty God works His miracles in mysterious ways." I touched his arm.

"There is a reason behind all this. We are being shown something to change lives. We are blessed to have been chosen … in our time – in your kingdom, Alfred."

With that impassioned defence from me, his bishop and family tutor, he lay back once more, sighed and propped his head in a cupped hand, the position I found him in. A king in pain. Inward and bodily. With his free hand he pointed a finger of disdain.

"Asser. Listen. They tell me you've emptied out the Roman House at Midelney and sent my monks back to France. Have you now become king of Wessex that you can do these things?"

"A murder in all but name, Alfred, in my church – a nest of vipers. I am their bishop, they were monks in my diocese. It was not a matter for a king."

"So you say. And what have you done with your lepers and saints?"

"Midelney was like a pig-sty. It has been cleaned from top to bottom by my Welsh friends and is now a Carmelite House with the leper hospice behind. Alwyn is the abbess, the Egyptian Emma her mentor, the convicted monks are bound to the hospice and to their abbess. It is a new beginning in Christ."

"Hmm. You are my closest friend and yet I do not understand your mind. Tell me … why a Carmelite Convent? Who ever heard of them in England?"

"God has shown me. I saw the barefoot grandchild protected by Elijah."

"Asser, you are a strange man! It is your Welsh upbringing. Half of you is still a druid!"

He laughed for the first time and sat up.

"Send your Egyptian surgeon to me. If anyone needs help, I do. I shall not survive another winter, my friend. Not as I am."

"She is within a vow of silence."

"She speaks to you. You must extend that. Send her to me before I have to journey again to Glastonbury and Winchester. Before the month is out. And tell her, Asser, that her king demands her presence before him!"

He spreads his hands in a much lighter manner then sets them back behind his head like a youth in a summer meadow.

"Now … enough of all this … read me some Tacitus."

I gather up the book from his table. 'The annals of Imperial Rome', and I began. It was like the old days back. 'When Rome was first a city, the rulers were kings …'

He closed his eyes. "I like this man's style. A Roman with some wit."

Thirteen

Second medical miracle

I am back home again after a long day – a walk that seemed longer as the sun left us. My mind is too active to be drawn into sleep. I shall tell you now about the event I withheld from Alfred, but no doubt he'll hear about it soon enough – the extraordinary happenings of last Sunday.

It was a bad beginning – to cut hay on the Sabbath, especially on St Augustine's Day.

And what a blessing from God that He sent to me on that fateful morning, Emma, to begin the confession towards the lifting of her vow.

We were sitting in the herb garden. It has at long last become much warmer, but taken an eternity to get there for now we are beyond Easter. This lovely garden is so aromatic, especially with a full sun on it, or after soft rains. It is old with mature plants, some of them going back out of recent memory and was the creation of the founder of this monastery, St Adhelm. But before that who can say, could it have first been laid out in Roman times?

I was thinking of my predecessor as we sat there before beginning. He was a wise, spiritual man, and a writer, who studied under Hadrian in 670 before going across to the Irish House at Malmesbury, coming to us at Sherborne in 705. He was certainly a much better author than I could ever be, though Tacitus would have smiled at his ornate Latin.

This herb garden has supplied our kitchens since his day. It has been slowly added to over the years by travelling brothers who brought to us new plants, new herbs from Aquitaine and from Hispania – Spain now – rosemary, garlic and basil. Into this quiet reflective moment a child burst in upon us and threw himself headlong at my feet.

"Father! Holy Bishop Lord Asser. It is my father! He has fallen asleep and no one can wake him."

After exclaiming this he burst into tears. A fragile child, thin and bony, not getting enough to eat in this cruel and unending winter. He is older than his years already, it shows in his voice. Sister Emma bent over the boy, helped him to his feet and sat him next to her on the bench. His pallor looked all the more against her dark southern colouring. I asked him to tell us more – and who he was.

"Eric, Holy Father."

"Dry your eyes now." I passed him a soft linen cloth. "Tell us why your father has fallen into such a deep sleep."

The boy was frightened, nervous and hesitant. He stared up into Emma's face.

"Please, Holy Saint of Healing … please come to my father."

She touched his head and spread her hands, surprised that he had come for her. Not understanding why. I had to explain.

"Eric, Sister Emma may not speak, she is under a vow. It is only to me and in private that she is allowed to say things."

As if disregarding me completely, he jumped down from the seat and tugged at her hand.

"Please, Holy Mother, you must come! Only you can save him!"

Clearly I shall have to try and unravel all of this. I touched his shoulder and drew him back towards us. He is close to tears again. Emma took his hand and held it.

I could see it comforted him. A little. "Now, that's better … tell us calmly without all this torrent of words what has happened.

Has your father died? If he has I shall of course come to him and say over him prayers."

"No, no … he breathes. Slow … and deep."

"Ah, thanks be to God. Has he been drinking ales and mead?"

"Not at all, Holy Father. Nothing like that. He's been working from daybreak in the hayfield, and he fell."

The boy suddenly held his head in his hands and if he'd been the one who had stumbled. "He hit his head on a stone."

An accident to the head. I could see Emma craning forward. Sharp and alert. That was the reason why the man couldn't be woken. Emma stood up, nodded as if to reassure him that she would indeed come to the father, right away. But where?

I asked him. "Where do you live, Eric?"

"In Yet Minster, Holy Father."

"Then you're a very lucky boy... we shall both come with you."

But I made him wait. I wanted to change my gown. Emma would need her box of devices from the convent.

As soon as we could we set out, Eric several strides ahead and looking back, anxious that we were not going faster. I called him back to my side.

"Eric, we need to know exactly what happened to your father." This is an unusual boy – an open solemn face, a certainty of manner and purpose, unafraid of bishops and lady saints. I may one day find a place for him with us.

"Father was ordered by his lord to work on the hay hides by the Leigh Stream."

"But surely there can't be any hay ready yet after only a few warm days?"

He looked at me as if I knew little of country matters.

"The grass is always longer there. It's sheltered and faces the sun. Our lord wanted it scythed and stooked."

"The man's a fool. No one stooks wet green hay."

"His horses have no fodder. The winter has been so long. My father slipped from a pile of it and hit his dead on a stone. He told us."

"Ah ..." I looked towards Emma. I could see she needed more. I continued.

"So ... the fall itself didn't knock all the senses out of him?"

"No, sir. He kept on working until the pains in his head got too much. And he was sick. Then he came home."

"And then?"

"Father fell onto his bed and no one could wake him up."

We entered Bradford where the nunnery is set against the abbey and waited there for Emma to join us with her box. The boy was fretting and impatient.

"Will the doctor be long, Father? They say in the village that it is the long sleep before death, that his spirit is waiting to rise up to God."

I placed my arm across his shoulder. "Sister Emma had to go into the convent for her special box. You may run on and say we are coming as fast as we can."

But he shook his head, eyes flooding once more with tears. He wants to stay with us. Emma arrived with her box slung from a shoulder and we hurried on. The sun had now passed midday and we were finding all this haste hot work. The Minster at Yet is a small chapel with clustering around it a circle of dwellings. There are no free men here – the families and their cottages are bonded to the Ceorl of Ryme Intrinseca, a man refused as a court reeve because of his bluster and unwillingness to study the Codes.

We found the injured man lying on a rush mat on the floor of his home. He had been turned onto his side to ease the breathing and secure the tongue. Around his head was bound a linen strip unstained by any blood. Emma hurried to him and bent low putting her ear to his mouth and chest, raising the lids of the sleeping man's eyes. She glanced at the assembled kin then whispered to me.

"Asser, I shall need again some hot coals."

The wife, Eric's mother, was distraught and knelt at her husband's side. I told her to bring us glowing coals in a fire-basket. To be given a task seemed to settle her. The look she gave the Egyptian surgeon was full of awe. My friend's reputation has travelled ahead of her.

Emma unwrapped the bandage with care, with the gentleness of a mother taking swaddling bands from a baby. She then felt the man's skull. He was sleeping so profoundly that he made no response, neither sigh nor murmur. Once again she raised the eyelids and seemed to look carefully into each one as if it held some answer for her. She called me over and spoke in a low voice.

"Ask the boy to leave us. I shall be quick. I shall need clean rain-water."

When the wife brought that, I thanked her and said to bring in the brazier of hot embers. The fire-basket was brought quickly and set down. The wife was frightened by all of this, and I confess so was I. Only the presence of her bishop convinced the woman that we were not practising magic. I told her to wait outside with Eric and to draw back the rush curtain to let in as much light as possible. Now alone, Emma opened her box and took from it her linen-roll of devices. She lifted out a sharp razor and a tubular instrument shaped like an hour-candle but not hollowed. I could see it had a sharp toothed end, but no point. Just as with John Saxon, these procedures set upon her an inward mood as if occupied by a force excluding everything except what she was about to do. The kind of self-absorption I have rarely witnessed before except in some seers in Aquitaine, wandering holy men that sat cross-legged in a tree's shade, trance-like.

Emma poured the spring water into one of her silver dishes and tipped granules into it which I recognised now as being salt. She then took some pellets of soft fabric and sponged a point above the man's left ear, halfway to the crown. Next the blade of her razor was passed through the fire-glow of the embers. She then shaved a disc on the scalp until it was bare. I caught my breath. A bruise was revealed. She worked swiftly as a shepherd does when shearing, then, as if she needed her tube to brand him with a slave-master's mark, she passed the tip of it through a flame. In a second movement she cut down with her razor. I turned away my eyes. But only for a moment. I was enwrapped by her skills and deftness. My heart was beating quickly, my mouth dry. The cut-down of the razor divided the scalp to the bone beneath. Dark spent blood oozed up. I was spell-bound. With her next action she did something amazing. She pressed down her tubular instrument onto the bare bone, then spun the reamer to and fro with great speed between the flat of her palms. Suddenly it gave way and she stopped at once, lifting out a plug of skull bone. She sliced the glistening covering with her razor. What outflowed was putrid black blood. It surged out freely and tracked down into her catching dish where it set like a jelly, a brawn, a stale gravy. And then, like the withdrawing of a living thing the brain drew back – the brain lining, mother of all membranes, slithering away like an eel in wet grass. She pressed the disc of bone back into its hole and set the scalp flap across it, pressing it down with two silver clips. Lastly she rewound, with delicacy and dexterity, the linen bandage.

The man's breathing changed suddenly from sighing to soft rhythms of sleep, then we could hear it no more. I prayed. Was he dead? But no – he called forth in a firm voice.

"Eric! Eric ... I'm cold! Bring me a blanket."

The second miracle was performed by this saintly, gifted woman touched by God. On which Battlefields she learned these wonders I cannot imagine – only from wars deep in Arabia. Not even the anatomists of Mantua or Milan would have dared to do what she has just done here in remote Wessex, in a village hut. For certain, had they tried outside their cities they would have been charged with blasphemy and magic.

Today we have been in the presence of Christ and the animus of Hippocrates.

FOURTEEN

The afflictions of Alfred

It will be said by some when they come to the end of these winter passages from Wessex, surely there must be a lot more to come? Of course there is, but it is not down to me to record it. This is but a personal indulgence, a way of passing through the longest and dreariest winter for many a year. It may also stand as a gift to my family at St David's – that they still remain in my thoughts and in my heart.

When I am done and summer arrives in all its healing warmth, I may return to these notes to add a post-scriptum. An old story I have been told and would not like it to become lost. It recalls those last days when Rome was withdrawing from a land it no longer regarded as inseparate from itself – Britannia. Forgive that wish of mine; it is not too much to ask, is it?

I am no historian. In that skill I rate very poorly – take my life of King Alfred. I never finished it. How could I … he still lives. We are going there tomorrow. His bishop and the Coptic Emma, saint of Mercy. Nor am I a natural writer like Tacitus, I do not have that depth of learning and wit. I see myself more as a painter of frescoes or the setter of a mosaic, a would-be craftsman who begins a task and does not finish it – always finding in it too many faults to satisfy. My sentences are often clumsy, my Latin archaic, my constructions untidy – but Alfred is pleased with my little volume about him, as well he might. No biographer is ever fully honest, only his retrospective colleagues, viewing a king's life in a bigger picture from a later age. I do gain in immediacy over those of later detachment and further scholarship. In this winter journal my readers may find surprises, some about Emma I have described, yet there are matters not yet for public viewing. I have written about Alfred's gifts and greatness – his other sides I have passed over, though I have inserted the episode of his beseeching prayer as a young man in Cornwall – to have his itch and anguish lifted, asking for a more manageable penance. Was that not a strange prayer? What descended was much worse and for which no help was ever found – no physician from Rome to Rochester could understand it, let alone offer treatment. Many were tried.

The heaviness and inward-searching mood of yesterday has left me and I'm ready for this new day of bright light and southern airs, ready for our walk to Montacute. And already I can see Emma walking towards me through our herb garden. Her step also is lighter. She holds her head higher. My window is open and she is aware of me looking down. I call to her.

"Good morning, Emma. Summer has arrived at last!"

I go down. I am delivering Emma today into the king's presence as commanded. Summer in Blackmoor Vale – how lovely it is when it breaks in on us all at once, almost omitting spring altogether. Of course, it is not a moor any longer, and the great forest of Selwood shrinks every year back onto itself. For 500 years sheep have grazed from Sherborne to Cerne and they have rounded the uplands to a smooth springing turf. The forests that were there for so long are now forgotten – it seems impossible to imagine that they once covered it all.

This is a morning made for walking, the air rich in soft scents brought in on a sea breeze from the south. It will cool us for the day's warmth is already upon us. Sebastian has been sent off ahead to say we're on our way. I shall not describe our walk only to say we paused at Odcombe where the Langport Way bears north to Ilchester and the great Roman road, the Fosse Way. Yet the wonder of the road and all the civilising way the Romans brought to us brings only to mind the sour comments made by Tacitus: 'The Britons call it civilisation when it was really just part of their servitude'. Of course, he likes these cutting asides, they please his father-in-law, Agricola. Well think of this – we are still here … and where now is the Roman Empire? Not anyway in Rome … far away to the East in the city of Constantine.

The sun is higher, the countryside magical. I am in love with this land of Wessex. Wales is my mother but this world around me now is as beautiful as a wife or daughter. The peaked hill at Montacute has been visible for a little while. As we come nearer I can see Sebastian talking with a group of Cluniac monks. Today we are escorted in by two different officials, men I don't know but their voices are rich in marshland spaces, eeling and fowling – faces weathered by winter winds and the sun's force thrown back by wide waters. We are led into the king's presence. It is a makeshift building more a shelter than somewhere to live. He has always had to be on the move with his warband, among his people – a man more at ease with plainness than palaces. The air within is stale. A slept-in odour. Alfred's eyes are heavy. He sleeps when the world outside has been awake as long as a midwinter's day. He is dressed in a winter tunic and wears coarse sandals on his feet. He sits on the edge of his night bench with a forward lean that might suggest a greeting or pain, or the examination of a rare visitor.

"So, Asser ... at last. And this is your Egyptian. I have been waiting a long time."

Emma genuflexes. Her eyes are on him. She is taking everything in – the odour of the room, the drawn reed screen across the sun, the lowness of his mood. Alfred doesn't rise, offer his hand or spirit but looks her up and down – in his eyes an irony. I suspect he has been awake most of the night and didn't sleep until the first fingers of dawn-light.

"No physician, Egyptian, has ever helped me. They have gone away with my bookmark and a light purse. But ..." he sits straighter and a fleeting smile passed through his lips gathering in the iron from his eyes, " I have heard you are descended from Merlin. That you have worked magic charms and strange methods upon my abbot John of Saxony. Indeed you saved his life with your needles and devices. And still more ... you have raised from a death-sleep a bond-man at Yet minster, removing indeed the blood-flux from his skull."

Emma rose to her feet and stepped back beside me. She has been allowed and granted for this meeting permission to speak.

"It is not magic, My Lord King Alfred, only a craft. Like the glaziers at the windows of your new Carmelite House."

"Ah … an answer to put me in my place. Very well, do what you will with me, I am ready. I know what to expect. I have read many times the Leech Book of Bald."

She looked away from him, away from his gaze. "My ways are different, My Lord. I follow no book."

Alfred looked at her for some time before replying.

"Perhaps. Are not some methods of cure even worse than the sickness itself? You are a crafts-woman … I like that. Trained fingers can be better than a mind full of fancy and theories. I like someone who works from experience – as you've told me my glaziers do."

Alfred is in darkness His voice sarcastic. "So what do you intend to inflict upon me first, Mistress Seamstress?"

"I must examine your body."

Alfred stares at me, yet I can see a change in his eyes – that of intrigue. "A woman to examine my body, Asser? What a bold woman! Can we allow that?"

"Careful observation is part of her method, Alfred."

"Do I want to be observed? You'd better stay with us. Listen and watch. Who knows what this woman of the Nile will do to me."

He instructed his thegns to draw back the night curtain. "I might be spirited away, Asser, down the Nile in a basket … it has happened before."

Emma looks to me. "I will wait outside, Asser. Let the king take off his clothes and cover his nakedness with a clean drape." She has now entered her calling and speaks like a master. Alfred's humour has gone. He has become sour.

"Not even Ealswith, my wife, has gazed upon every part of me, Physician."

I've had enough of this.

"Her name is Emma, Alfred, or Sister Emma. She is a healing master and has a name as good as yours."

He knows that. And respects her directness and gifts. The technique is strange, and he is making a fuss.

"Very well. A sick man has no honour in the presence of doctors."

Emma feels in her bag and draws out a beaker. She passed it to me.

"Please ask King Alfred to set some of his urine in here." And with that she left us.

Both Alfred and I are now truly dismayed. To ask a king to piss for you is like asking Alexander the Great to move so he may cast no shadow on Diogenes. It falls to me to wave away the remaining thegn. When alone, I explain.

"Better do what she says, Alfred. This is a remarkable woman. I watched her drill the man's skull and tap off the spent blood. I saw him wake up and ask for a blanket."

He takes the beaker with disgust and reluctance. "Well ... there are worse things, I suppose. I am not usually asked for piss. It costs little, only a measure of shame. Go out, Asser. I can't piss with you standing over me."

I went outside to join Emma. She was looking down at the dark-gowned monks, watching Sebastian helping and holding their measuring cords. For a man who has run nine miles, he has the lightness of step of a Welsh mountain goat. I asked her to sit beside me on an ancient lichened block.

"Emma, shall I tell you something of the king's childhood ... might that help?"

She doesn't look at me but keeps a distance. For all her watching the measuring beneath us, I feel her thoughts are much far#ther from me than that.

"Yes. Tell me, Asser."

"I can only be brief. We will be called back soon." I look behind us towards the rounded construction that passes for Alfred's home, spread my hands and begin.

"First – I believe he was the most favoured of the children, the most loved by his mother Osburh, the most admired by his father Aethelwulf. His father took him to Rome when he was still very small, only four years old. That must have been a painful separation for the child, and for the mother who adored him. Not long after they safely came back his mother was overwhelmed by a sickness, a deep lethargy and the sweating signs which are heralds, the messengers of death. It is not unlike that which Alfred suffers with today, and the bitter memory of her suffering fills him with dark thoughts and sour humours. Death, he imagines, is like the great hound of Molossia – it searches and hunts him down."

Emma said nothing. She listens intently, no longer drawn into far-away lands and bad memories of her own. Sebastian sees us and waves, sends towards us a smile from his heart. He is happy. I continue.

"When his mother died the little boy was heart-broken. There followed a period of mourning until finally his father decided to take the boy back to the Pope for comforting. Off they went again, a vast and endless journey that took for ever. But they eventually arrived safely and Alfred was anointed by the Pope himself, as a future king – a boy of seven with older brothers ahead of him in precedence. How strange, and yet how prophetic. Was it part of God's design? Who can say?"

Just then the king's reeve came out and waved us back in. He is a presumptive servant to use a gesture like that over us. A fisherman or fowler. We are not his dogs.

"I shall continue with our story, Emma, on the way home. There is a dark side to it. One of his brothers entered the step-mother's bed. I believe Alfred carries all that in his heart."

Alfred was lying flat covered with a white sleep-sheet. He dismissed the reeve.

"You've been a long time. It's always the same with physicians – to be kept waiting is part of the penance."

He is uneasy and fearful, yet in battle the bravest of leaders. The story of the skull piercing has shocked and terrified him. Emma said nothing. She went to him and folded down the sheet so that only the groin and his manhood remained covered. She felt his neck, armpits and belly, pushing down deeply with her fingertips, asking if it caused pain. He made no answer but the pain in his eyes was not from that. Emma then tapped him like a cooper with a barrel, listening to the resonance or absence of it. The same with his chest. In a sudden single movement she raised the sheet and examined his manliness, turned him over and paused. She could see, even as I could, the scalded skin around his arse from scratching. But that wasn't all. She sat him up and indicated he must put out his tongue. Moments later she pulled down his lower eyelids to see what they would tell her. It was the performance of a master. Finally she covered him with the bedding and crossed to the table where he had left the beaker of urine. I watched entranced. She decanted some into a conical flask and held it up to the sunlight as if the colour of it might give her an answer. She then dipped the tip of her little finger into the piss and tasted it. For sweetness. I have heard of that but never seen it done. My heart was beating quickly. I have never witnessed a physician, a woman, do such things to a man – a king. Had I not seen already the miracles she has done I would have suspected her of wizardry and secret rites. In all it had taken her no more than a quarter of an hour. She works with the swiftness of the shepherd with a new-born lamb. Finally she beckoned me and we left him to recover his composure.

"So, Emma … I am greatly impressed. But can you tell me now after all that what is wrong with my king? I am astonished he allowed you to examine him in so strange a way."

She answered at once, as if she had known all along. "King Alfred has a melancholia, a blackness of bile. I shall cure him, if he listens."

The reeve summoned us once more. His gestures are tiresome. We found Alfred dressed and seated on a bench. The room remained in full sunlight, the withy still tied back.

"So, my strange Egyptian, what will you order for your sick pharaoh?"

"My Lord, you have been in the grasp of a deep melancholia. But I am able to cure it."

He said nothing, but there came no contradiction of protest. He looked from her to me. Her shaft of diagnosis has bitten deep and hard. Perhaps he too had known it already. His manner was now quiet as if far away in some other place.

"It seems I can be cured, Asser, like our John of Saxony, like your senseless man with too much blood on his brain."

His sigh was from the heart, from deep in his past, from years of suffering and sleeplessness.

"You have found for me a remarkable woman … who is to cure me."

He turned his gaze back on Emma, eyebrows lifted in enquiry.

"And how shall this take place?"

"You must listen to what I say, King Alfred. Certainly you will die otherwise."

"I am listening to you, Emma of Grace." He has used her name for the first time, and with great courtesy.

"Please give me your treatments. I know that as I am I shall not live through another bitter winter."

She is now master of him, and of her craft. "Please do not interrupt me as I tell you what you will have to do to return into God's harmony."

"Am I not attentive?" He points to me. "Asser, my friend, this woman is like the queen of the Iceni, except that she knows the pyramids better than the walls of Colchester. I should be glad if she didn't employ a scorpion. I do not wish to suffer like Cleopatra."

I spread my hands to stop him – not a gesture to be used upon a king, hardly even to check a friend.

"Alfred … how can you be so much the sceptic. Emma is the best physician ever to come to Wessex. I know. I have seen it. Two men live who would be dead had God not sent her to us. Listen to what she says as a man in need. As the third man she shall heal."

He shrugs and offers a wry smile. "Have I not already said I am listening?"

With no further ado she launches into his healing penance.

"Alfred, you must run five miles a day with Sebastian."

How could I not smile at that. The penalties for admitted illness are Sybilline but far from harsh. Alfred exploded. Even that was a good sign.

"What! Run! Are you mad? I can barely leave my bed!"

"My Lord. You must run off your melancholia. Discharge the black bile through your sweat."

He stares at me in utter disbelief. "I am ill and she wants to whip me for it, Asser!"

But Emma continued, unrepentant and unhearing.

"Next, you must hand over the kingship to your son Edward within two years and spend what remains of your life in simplicity. Like a Carmelite. You should translate the psalms of David into words your people can understand."

At that he jumped to his feet. "Great Heavens … can this be

right, Asser – or am I the one who is already mad? I have to run like Pheidippedes and study like Bede?"

"Yes." I said.

He hurried to the window and threw back the blinds to their limit. The sun poured down on him. He was a man lit up like an icon in Byzantium. Surely God's light and blessing is striking and entering him. When he turned to us there existed for the first time a new tranquillity in his eyes.

"Very well. It is to be then. Call up my running master Sebastian. I shall need a summer tunic and soft sandals."

FIFTEEN

Emma's confession

Time has moved on, summer and yet more winters. I am able to write this down now. I know I shall be criticised for betraying a confession. I am the author of these notes and bear that responsibility; no writer can leave a story unfinished even if it brings down upon his head abuse. It is the penalty of authorship. In my defence I can offer up this – Emma has returned to Egypt. She has been called back to Rosetta by royal messenger, back to tend to the lepers she left to come to me to lift her oppressive vow. And should this book – it has become that – ever be read in some distance future, all of us, except Alfred, will be forgotten, and of no importance.

The tap on my door is Sebastian with my breakfast. He draws up a small table to my desk and sets down the tray. His smile is affectionate, and ironic.

"Writing again, Asser. Are we into St Michael's Mass already?"

He is right. I do take up my quill to banish winter from my rooms, my eyes and my mind. "Is there still something left to say?"

We are together. This is a strange room for a confession. We are not in half darkness with a grill and a priest on the far side murmuring.

"Let us begin, Emma. Just as it comes to you. I am listening."

She nods. "I was born in St Lo, in Normandy. Yet my parents were from the mountains. My father was a cook and they had left their home and land to come down and serve the Dukes of Normandy. I was the fifth child in a family of seven – five brothers and two girls. We were so poor that my mother would go down every day to the castle kitchens and bring back for us scraps thrown aside for pigs. Do you know, St Lo, Asser?"

"No."

"The Northmen, violent, greedy and stupid men wanted it. Attacked us to capture our town. Yet it was a fortress. We thought we were safe from them. Our hill rises above the river. It is steep. We imagined no one could scale that wall. Its base was in deep water. But these men were not stupid about warfare. They were cunning. They came at us during the night when there was no moon and threw up ladders. That part of the ramparts was undefended. It had always been secure. They came over, killed, burned and raped. A mayhem of fire and screaming."

She stopped. A tremor had taken over her shoulders and hands – tears welled up into her eyes. I waited. There will be much more. Very much more.

"I was a child of thirteen, Asser. What could I do? Our family was spared. Three of my brothers were taken as slaves but the little ones were untouched. They had no need to kill my father, he was only a cook. The soldiers looked at me. I knew that look but I was skin and bone, not fit for a man. I, too, was spared. Then things quietened down. Camp followers came in through the open gates. Our town was sacked – into the ruins came traders, women, magicians and tumblers, people who profited by the misfortunes of others. My mother sold me to an Arab, a healer, a man who followed the Vikings for business, selling his skills to any victim who could find his fee. Imagine; a child sold by her own mother. Only a thing, an object in her eyes – money to feed the little ones. I no longer blame her. How much was I worth, a thin, ragged waif – a few coins. But I am full of anger, Asser."

"Yes." She does not weep. This is woman who has never allowed herself to do so.

"My Arab master took me to Alexandria. It was a long journey. We travelled from town to town. I was dressed as a boy to avoid comments and trouble. He began to teach me his skills with herbs and remedies and how to pass him his instruments. My master had two horses – one for himself and the other for his boxes of medicines and devices. I ran alongside. At first, in the evenings when we finally stopped, I would fall and faint – but slowly I became used to it – running every day. When we reached the hot country of the south he put up an Arab tent, and one night ... he drew me into his bed. A child. I was brutalised."

She came to a stop, stood up and crossed to my window. I thought we should end this confession for that day – her emotions were violent. Her whole body shook. But she didn't want that and after an interval came back to her chair, no longer trembling.

"I began to swell. I was with child, a girl not yet fourteen. I hated him for it. Despised him; not only for that, but for the way he fed like a wolf on the pleading of my people – sick children, dying babies, the lame and the sightless – all would come. For a fee."

She held her head in her arms. I placed my hand on her shoulder. "It is all in the past. So long ago. You are here with us, Emma, and admired. Rest a while before you tell me the rest of this cruel story."

The silence was longer this time. Suddenly she continued, not looking at me – out of the window.

"He taught me more, the secrets of his craft – how to flame knives so that there was no putrefaction, to soak instruments in boiling water so they do not place upon open flesh the humours of decay. There was something else, a gift which also healed – a way of listening."

"Yes."

"I drowned my baby, Asser. He was so beautiful, so tender and innocent. I should have drowned myself at the same time for such blasphemy and wickedness. My master found out. Someone had seen me. I was beaten with rods, whipped and left for dead. But I lived. Crawled away. Lived as an outcast, shunned and despised. Why was I kept alive – was there a purpose? Where could I go except to the lepers of Rosetta."

She has dropped to her knees in front of me, her forehead resting on the floor. I said this over her. A redemption.

"Emma, the Lord our Saviour forgives those who are truly repentant. I have no more penances for you; you have suffered for so long and carried all this pain with you in your heart, night and day, wherever you go. You have sinned, and been sinned against. The life you took had no guilt, an innocent formed in the image of God, but his spirit is not mortal. Your child is with Jesus. I bless you for the life you have chosen, for your compassion and courage. You were saved for a purpose, and you have found it."

I placed my hand on her head.

"In some ways, Emma, you are no different from Saul who ordered the stoning of Stephen, and like him you have been shown the true way. Jesus says: 'I am the Way, the Truth and The Light.' He would rather accept the love of a sinner than all the prayers of the righteous. You were only a child, and you acted like a child. I lift your guilt. The loss of one life has been the gift of life to many others, just as our Saviour gave His life on the Cross for us. Jesus said to Mary: 'Go, and do not sin again.' I remove your vow of silence and bless you for coming to us.

In nomine Patris, Filius et Spiritus Sanctus. Lord, bless Thy servant Emma, that she may be a delight to you, always."

And now the tears flow.

My door is opening. It is Sebastian.

"Asser? You weep ... are you all right? Your breakfast is cold. Shall I bring some more?"

SIXTEEN

No story

897 AD June 11th: St Barnabas the Apostle

No story ever has an ending. It is a play. Actors leave the boards and another cast will enter another time to retell the mysteries. Several years have now passed by and over me. I have come to love this land more and more – my Sherborne, my life here with my brothers. Yet I know deep down that God will ask me to come to Him before my hair becomes fully white.

Alfred has translated his kingship to his first born Edward the Elder, and he now lives in the Carmelite House and Hospice at Midelney. He has made a close friendship with Alwyn and there is a true affection between them. The ages do not separate them – their kindred spirits have brought them close. There exists a tenderness that passes from one to the other in each direction, and that is rare. I have often seen and heard it. I have known men who have only found that love and companionship with their dog or horse. Every morning Sebastian goes over to see them and Alfred has come to show pleasure in my young athlete who runs daily with him. And he himself has become a changed man, as any man might who has been cured of a painful and lowering sickness. He keeps his feet bare in the tradition of the calling, and he too has become an athlete, quick of eye and mind, firm of flesh. Does he not embrace Juvenal's dictum, encouragement ... 'You should pray to have a sound mind in a sound body ... *mens sana in corpore sano.*'

Simple words but true. Our old Welsh couple are alive and continue to work from dawn to dusk in the gardens restoring them to fruitfulness, something not seen there since the last Roman veteran died. There is a weathered grave now cleared and edged in small flowers: 'Amatus Clavian aet XC.' A great age for those days. Only a gardener with a tranquil mind can have lived so long. Our Welsh gardeners have become watchful and careful, mindful of sharp stones that will injure their unfeeling hands and feet and cause fresh sores. Three other lepers have joined them – two women and a child – and they have been made welcome. The hospice has still its slave – my monk Oswald on a suspended death sentence. He does all their cooking, cleaning, peeling and preparing the garden vegetables, for his charges have clumsy hands. He also does all their dressings and applies Emma's balm, a soothing preparation that Alfred himself says is giving him heartfelt relief and better nights. Oswald is a changed man, quite possessive about the five people in his care and appears to have adopted a role for himself, a hospice under-abbot. He has acquired heights of responsibility and caring he could never have glimpsed in his old resentful and coarser ways. Nor has he caught the whitening sickness, and has no fears of doing so. He believes that God has given him back a life of purpose. I am glad I did not order his hanging – what a waste and stupid cruelty that would have been, an insult to Christ my Redeemer and Saviour.

The youth so evilly led astray, Amatus, has grown into a fine young man and remains under Sister Alwyn's wise and guiding hands. More than that he has been taken on as Alfred's pupil and introduced to philosophers, history and the ways of Rome. Also he has discovered a gift for music and has learned the harp from Alwyn, and the sad songs of my homeland. Furthermore he sits daily with Alfred in the scriptorium as his teacher translates the Psalms of David into our English language.

I have consecrated the east end of the barn for the House chapel and it has now a new east window as well as an altar table brought down from Winchester. I led the Mass of sacred dedication and offered up prayers in the name of Grace, Healing, Refuge and Elijah. We processed and sang one of the newly translated psalms, the first one to be completed by Alfred, Psalm 23. Our young Frankish trainee played on the harp music he had composed for the day, as well as beautiful words. The white gowns, the bare feet, the soft music, the poetry, brought tears flooding into my eyes. It seemed at that moment God was amongst us – and his Son, the greatest of all healers.

As for me, I have one final task – to bring this small book to its conclusion. I hope to delay tying the tapes around it for a little bit longer – the slightest of my works yet in its way the one closest to my heart.

My life is as always busy. It is warming and satisfying that I am blessed with good companions, health, a good appetite and easy sleep. I have become proud of Sebastian. Alfred wants to send him to Rome as he was for a papal blessing that he might and should carry on this diocese as an island of faith and learning in the future. But I have stayed Alfred's hand. I don't think he's quite ready yet – and I want to have him by my side for the year or two still allotted to me. He has much to learn from Alfred and myself before that. I shall make him a suffragan bishop when the time is right for so vast and dangerous a journey.

I do not wish to close this part on a note of sadness reflecting on the passage of time, of lives ending. I hope to set down other matters as they arise. For the moment I shall end here to reflect upon a thought heavy in my mind – that there is such a need for all of us to accept each other. There are no differences, no faults, no sicknesses, no guilt that separates us from the love of God. How can we not accept each other when we are all so loved – surely that is the way forward. There is no other way.

       Thanks be to God
       Sherborne in the year of Our Lord, 897.

Author's notes and thoughts

I have called this piece a two-part invention so that I offer up a caution – whilst much of it is fact, more is fiction. For example, the arrival, nature, skills and character of Emma sit in the former ... an invention. The attempted murder of John Saxon is a recorded fact.

The afflictions of King Alfred are those listed by Asser himself. No diagnosis was ever made and it remains a mystery to this day. Perhaps it was a bowel disorder. Some scholars think so. Asser has written a biography of King Alfred, a unique creation for those days where so little has been handed down, though the Anglo-Saxon Chronicles survive. Most of this book stems from Asser's 'Life of Alfred.'

The name Asser is intriguing and may well derive from the Hebrew named Asher, the 7th son of Jacob. It is a name still heard, in various forms. When the Romans left Britain they achieved amongst their communities a high level of literacy, and it was a burning wish of Alfred's to bring education back into his people. And scholars were arising, books written again – Bede was one of the greatest scholars of his time in Western Europe and his history – *The ecclesiastical history of the English people*, a light in a shadowy age. St Adhelm, bishop of Sherborne 150 years before Asser was also a writer. His work was in Latin.

The Somerset Levels I know well from boyhood – from many fishing expeditions near Athelney and Langport. It was there that I saw my first bittern, a flat and desolate place that always seems to me to exist in winter clothing – in its ancient drainage canal I caught my first tench and learned how to unhook eels.

My thanks go out to modern authors, historians:

Sir Frank Stenton: *Anglo-Saxon England.* I found it moving, memorable, a work of love and scholarship, an easy style which places him for me in the company of Tacitus, William Warde Fowler and Sir Charles Oman.

Who's who in Roman Britain and Anglo-Saxon England: R. Fletcher, Shepherd-Walwyn.

Tacitus: *The annals of Imperial Rome.*

William Warde Fowler: *Julius Caesar.*

Charles Oman: *England before the Norman Conquest.*

And Asser's own book within *Alfred the Great.* Penguin Classic, 1983.

And to three remarkable wives:

Lady D.M. Stenton who edited the final draft of *Anglo-Saxon England.*

My own wife Ann who reads and edits my work and without whose love and support no books would have been written.

Thirdly – King Alfred's wife Ealswith. Why she didn't feature in Asser's biography is a mystery. Perhaps they didn't get on, perhaps Asser was critical of her not being at her husband's side throughout – a husband she must have found difficult with his moods, introspection, warband and an education far beyond her own.

Alfred's final years are also a mystery. Asser did not finish his biography, nor are those final years mentioned so far as I know in the Anglo-Saxon Chronicles. Like Diocletian, he resigned the leadership, but not three ways. He died on October 26th 899, but where he lies now is quite unknown.

I leave with some reluctance having relived scenes so well known to me in Somerset and Dorset, and having shared with Alfred a vast journey at the age of four. Alfred's jewel, a gold ring inscribed 'Alfred made me' is a treasure: I would like to think Somerset did the same for me, impressing a child already part-forged in a land where he spent five years in bare feet.

London, Dollis Hill Lane April 2005 – February 2018